A CHANGE OF LUCK

Jackie McLeod

PublishAmerica
Baltimore

© 2010 by Jackie McLeod.
All rights reserved. No part of this book may be reproduced, stored in a retrieval system or transmitted in any form or by any means without the prior written permission of the publishers, except by a reviewer who may quote brief passages in a review to be printed in a newspaper, magazine or journal.

First printing

All characters in this book are fictitious, and any resemblance to real persons, living or dead, is coincidental.

PublishAmerica has allowed this work to remain exactly as the author intended, verbatim, without editorial input.

Hardcover 978-1-4512-2587-7
Softcover 978-1-4512-2588-4
PUBLISHED BY PUBLISHAMERICA, LLLP
www.publishamerica.com
Baltimore

Printed in the United States of America

Dedicated to my husband for encouraging me to write after so many years of telling me I couldn't spell. I love you Steve; also, dedicated to my friends and family.

TABLE OF CONTENTS

In the Beginning 9
Called to the Office 13
The Suspension 19
Drowning Our Sorrows 35
Detour on the Road Home 47
All about David 51
Back on the Road 55
Montgomery, Alabama 59
The New Comer 65
The Chase Begins 71
On to the Beach 77
Fantasies 81
David Arrives 91
Fun-n-wet 97
Nick Was Late With his Report 113
At the Beach 115
The Sea Plane Ride 117
Back in Montgomery Again 121
Friday Night at John's by the Sea 125
Tracy 129
Nick's Spiritual Experience 133
The Finding 143
Men Watch the News 147
Trying for an Interview 153
Abby Meets Granny 159
We Finally Catch Up 173
A Late Dinner 181
Sunday Morning 189
The Reveal 197
Mr. Durrell 203
Biloxi 209

David on the Run 215
Biloxi night 217
Weddings in the Family 225
Back to Aviation World 229
Nelly 235
Three Years Later 239

CHAPTER 1

In the beginning

"And the mysterious black sedan sat outside *Aviation World* awaiting for the "subject" to exit the building," Nick breathed the words out in one breath while sitting in the driver's seat of the parked Chevy Impala; meanwhile he impatiently drummed his fingers on top of the leather steering wheel to the beat of a popular song playing loudly on the radio. He had forgotten how much patience it took to follow "subjects," he thought as he stopped his drumming and hung his hand out the window. His window was open to let in the cool spring air in hopes to overcome the nature of any black sedan while sitting in the sun; the color black absorb the heat like a sponge as the unforgiving noon sun approached it's pentacle in the sky. He promised himself that next time he would buy a white car regardless of the anonymity of the vehicle. He didn't feel it appropriate to leave the car running for hours in an effort to afford the luxury of cool air-conditioning, so he frugally suffered the heat with the window open.

It was a stroke of luck that Private Detective Nick Barkowski was able to procure a lucrative account during these hard economic times—the job came with an offer that would keep his doors open for another month or two and also pay his extensive advertizing expenses for the next year.

The account made up for at least twenty-five of his usual accounts. Those accounts consisted of fanatical investigations into the wills of decedents with low end estates and poor estate planning. Even though they were not exciting cases, they were his "bread and butter." Unlike this case, when investigating financial information all Nick had to do was a few magical clicks of the computer mouse over the internet and vela all the whereabouts of money, properties and assets were revealed. Then his secretary would print, scan and email the desired information to his clients; it usually took only a couple of hours. Very few assets now-a-days were left undocumented in pubic data bases. His reputation was impeccable and his cliental vast.

By specializing in estate inventory investigations, he liked to believe that he was contributing toward helping the innocent who could no longer speak for themselves—they were the recently deceased who wanted their precious valuables to go to their rightful heirs. Although estate investigations were Nick's "bread and butter," they paid less per quota and weren't as challenging.

The request for field work came from a lawyer whose client was willing to pay more than Nick expected or asked. Nick's client found Nick the easy way, which was through a search on the internet with the keywords investigator and Atlanta, Ga. Nick's URL was third on the list as simpleinvestigations.com but first in a promise to be affordable. After a brief background check of Nick's company, an attorney form Casper, Wyoming, being impressed with Nick's work, negotiated a staggering price larger than Nick would have expected.

Nick was nature's genetic answer to what happened when two different races marry. He was perfect in most every way. He had the naturally lean body, smooth olive completion, high cheek bones and straight black hair inherited from his Native American mother; but he also had the straight nose and handsome Russian features of his father. Although, he was a union of both races, he mostly looked Native American. Curiously, he had one light brown eye and one blue eye and used colored contacts to match them; some days he had blue eyes and some days he had brown eyes. Oddly enough, before Nick decided to become a private detective, he had graduated from medical school on a swim scholarship and became a doctor. Then a few years later, being a natural born general practitioner, he felt he'd been born too late. The old fashioned general practitioner idea of treating the whole patient was gone and was replaced by specialties—and plastic surgeons. Medical doctoring had become an emotionally charged and compliantly competitive environment where there was no place for intuitively smart doctors; each decision for a treatment had become based on written standard practice procedures and charts that were not applicable to every individual. Also, it was frustrating times where new discoveries in medical science were held to small leaps instead of big bounds by politics and money grubbing drug companies. Doctors feared law suites and became too tentative rather than aggressive in diagnostic decisions; the last true cure was discovered during World War II when penicillin was invented. However, the final decision was when his wife, Red Feather, died in childbirth and for all the medical technology no one was able to save her, not even himself. It left a bitter taste in his mouth.

When he buried Red Feather, he followed the Native American traditions for their daughter's sake; but, being half white he never had gotten in touch with his Native American side. He never had the spiritual event that all his Native American cousins had—which prompted names in the English translation such as Running Horse or Eagle Feather—he liked just Nick and liked being half white, the name his father gave him was just fine to him. Even still, his mother never gave up hope that Mother Nature would give him a name by a life changing event.

While he waited, he thought that he would have time to chew on a peanut butter sandwich and sip a cold can of coke from his cooler. He'd prefer a Coors Beer but he didn't drink on the job. After his lunch every day, the Private Detective called his client at the appointed time and each time the report was the same—which was unchanging and nothing significant. The subject conducted her life like any other working stiff—

much like an unnoticed drone bee mixing with thousands of other worker bees buzzing around a honeycomb. He was curious why a gentleman from another part of the United States and another lifestyle would want this woman followed. What was so special about her?

He picked up the phone and called the number to make an accounting of the last twenty-four hours. A female voice answered and Private Detective Nick Barkowski asked for Mr. Durrell. In contrast to the usual protocol of reporting to the lawyer, the lawyer asked Nick to report directly to his client.

Mr. Durrell voice came strong and clear over the cell phone as he asked, "Well, what is it today, son?"

"The subject spent the last twenty-four hours like the previous twenty-four hours. At 6:00 a.m. she stopped at Duncan-Doughnut and bought a black berry smoothie and a vegan flat bread breakfast sandwich......" Nick went through the routine detail by detail while wondering why this all was of interest to Mr. Durrell; perhaps she was on old mistress. Nick had followed mistresses upon occasion. Mr. Durrell hung on to every word like it was the most interesting story one could tell.

CHAPTER 2

Called to the Office

The sunlight showed brightly through the large full length window of the Atlanta office; it was as if the sun was trying to portray itself as a square spotlight on a theatrical stage. Open vertical blinds made shadowy diagonal lines on the adjacent wall. A woman on her daily lunchtime walk was framed in the window as she crossed opposite the small parking lot of the last grayish building of the large Logistic Park. In contrast to the other buildings, this building faced the woods; which was first was lined with Bradford Pears in snowy white bloom and then it progressed to mysterious pine green darkness. The other buildings faced mostly empty loading docks. The women's pink flowered dress and short blond hair lifted softly in a gentle breeze. She looked peaceful and happy walking amongst the glimpse of bright spring colors. It was all in sharp contrast to the sounds of the commercial aircraft only a few hundred feet above as they came in for a landing at the nearby Atlanta-Hartsfield International Airport.

As Nelly sat across the polished wooden desk waiting for her boss to enter his office, she turned her attention away from the women outside the window to the neatly framed posture of a Eurocopter flying against the blue summery sky. Its propeller blades were moving so fast that only wide transparent circles appeared where the blades should have been; it sported a cherry red fuselage. The blades on the tail were imbedded like a tire in an open wheel well or a box-fan in a case. Although Nellie had handled many helicopter parts and components over the years, she had never actually ridden in one. She harbored a secret fantasy to learn how to fly some day; however, given her middle age condition, she doubted that she would ever have the pleasure. These days she only had time to fight her middle age spread with a daily jog and her lifelong habit of taking on more responsibilities than she could manage, all in hopes that maybe someone would someday recognize her as useful and important, now that her children had grown the need to be needed was worse.

Nelly's job was to ensure that the invoices, the yellow certificates and the white calibration cards were completed; then again to ensure the paperwork was in perfect condition before being wrapped around various units, like altimeters and gyros,—and sent via air freight to high paying customers who could afford either a plane or a fleet of planes.

She had an eye for detail and truly, in all practicality, her creative mind was wasted on a clerical job. It was her co-workers that felt that way, not herself. However, having married young and having children young made it difficult for her to set high goals for her career; she made no excuses for herself because other women had accomplished their goals after having children. Being just twelve years from retirement, she was satisfied with her station in life. Earlier in life, before she became caught up with priorities that pulled her into the ordinary rather than that the extraordinary, she had started her first year of college with scholarships and a future toward nursing school. She had hoped that her retirement would be filled with traveling the world in the satisfaction of missionary work. She had always intended on going back but time had a way of running away from her/or everyone, as a matter of fact. However in all honesty, although clerking was hard and boring work, which required focus, she loved it. She found that she loved computers too and they had become her first priority these days.

A CHANGE OF LUCK

The business of repairing, or overhauling old aircraft parts (some as old as fifty years) was lucrative during hard economical times; mostly because customers didn't want to replace their old aircrafts with newer, more expensive, aircrafts. She was glad to be a part of a business that was doing well considering that the present unemployment rate was above eight percent and getting worse under the new President. *Aviation World* was still making a low two percent profit, but a profit just the same.

Still waiting for her boss, she squirmed in her hard metal chair and reached up to tug at a heavy ash colored bun in the back of her head. Tugging at her bun was a nervous habit she picked up over the years; along with twisting a strand of hair that loosely fell around her ear. It was usual for her to mess with her hair when nervous. Growing her hair long was the only free spirited statement she had left from her hippy days; now her life was formal and tightly structured, besides David, her husband, loved it. Her waist length light brown hair was usually left to hang loose, with the exception of work or church; then she would wrap it up in various twists. Her friend Kimberly from the church once giggled that Nelly had "uppity hair styles"…literally.

Squirming again Nelly wondered if she had time to go to the bathroom before her boss arrived. She had been here long enough for nature to call and she really wanted to answer, she supposed it was nerves. Instead Adam Wooddale answered the question when his tall, dark, frame walked through the door and sat in the black leather chair behind his desk; as he sat down the chair complained with a leathery squeak. From the expression on his face, she felt her mood turn grey, as grey as the paint on the walls; this isn't good she thought. A fleeting thought deep in the back of Nelly's mind hoped that this meeting was about receiving an "at-a-boy" or maybe even a long overdue raise. That thought was put to rest as Mr. Wooddale placed his hands on his desk and leaned forward; a motion that always expressed a change was about to come and he was bracing himself before he had to deliver the bad news.

Cautiously he began his delivery, "Nellie we need to make some changes that are vital to the company's operation and image."

Nelly just stared at him with her steal blue eyes in hopes that she wouldn't disgrace herself with the more urgent need to use the restroom; and also in hopes that he wouldn't notice that she was pinching her butt together. He seemed to take her frown as a non-verbal sign that she was preparing for an argument, rather than "please let's get this over quickly, I got to go to the bathroom." Nelly once saw on the educational channel where a famous actor said that he just acted as if he had to go to the restroom when the situation required that he needed to look in pain or angry, she couldn't remember the actor.

"I'm going to move you and Tracy out to the warehouse for awhile; then bring Heather and Sarah in to train for your positions," he said as he looked down at his hands not wanting to look her in her eyes any longer. That's what the employees called him, "ole shifty eyes."

Nellie sat up in her chair, mentally willing him to look back at her before interjecting, "Mr. Wooddale, I'm really terrible sorry about this…but I have to go take a shit!" Something inside her just didn't care anymore what she said to him, it seemed that he was always calling her in with bad news, never good news?

"What did you say?" he didn't trust his ears?

"Mr. Wooddale, Adam, please excuse me, I have to go… well, take a shit," she repeated as she shot the words over her shoulder and ran out of the office. After leaving a shocked Adam Wooddale with his mouth hanging open, she ran down the hall toward the bathroom in hopes that she wouldn't embarrass herself before she arrived. Perhaps this was a nervous condition she thought, he shouldn't have left me there so long.

This wasn't the conversation that he expected and it was uncharacteristic of Nelly. He had purposely called Nelly to his office and made her wait there for a few minutes in order to set up the psychological effect of his authority. He hoped that it would set her off balance so that she would be speechless but instead he was the one who was speechless. The shock of what just happened had blown all his best laid plans of intimidation; now he just sat there in a catatonic state, wondering what to do next. In jest, what appeared to be a sweet middle aged woman, who looked like she should be holding a china cup at Sunday tea, surprised him by revealing to him that she in essence had to take a "shit?"

He just sat there wondering what had just happened; or rather what just hadn't happen. By the time he had gathered himself together and looked for Nelly out in the hall, the hall was empty. He grinned to himself; Nelly had never failed to surprise him with her intellectual verbiage and knack for well chosen industrial buzz words, she even had failed to surprise him with her sometimes humorous quotes from old movies and her constant computer jargon but he had never expected the "drunken sailor on a Saturday night" vocabulary. He knew Nelly was very direct vocally but he never knew she cussed. He knew she lived a hard life. Her husband was hard on her, her grown children were hard on her and her job was hard on her; however his conscious didn't really bother him to deliver the bad the news—he had to do what he had to do as the owner of *Aviation World* demanded. He spoke out loud. "Ok, what do I do now," he said as he started walking down the hall after her. He didn't really want to lose Nelly as an employee, mostly because she was the go-to person when it came to fixing computer software. It wasn't that they didn't have an I.T. person; it was that she was practically a genius in integrating computer technology with shortening work processes and she didn't come with a consultant free.

CHAPTER 3

The Suspension

As Nelly ran down the narrow hall, Steve Jones from the indicator shop saluted her military style. Steve was the best looking male technician in the company and, thinking Nellie was old enough to get away with it, she relentlessly teased him.

She gave him a weak smile and a quick flirtatious wink as she passed his thick muscular frame.

His green eyes looked a little worried as Nelly rushed by. He was five years her junior but he appreciated her good looks and jovial nature; however, right now, she didn't seem too happy.

Leaving Steve behind, she continued running down the front hall past the generator shop and the airspeed shop to the vestibule in front of the ladies room. Nellie stopped for a brief moment to modestly check to see if anyone was following her before entering through the bathroom door. All she saw was an abandoned paper cup sitting on the water fountain and all she heard was the rumble of voices coming from the break room across the hall. Determining that she had the bathroom to herself, she pushed her way through the bathroom door and stormed the stall.

Regardless, to Nellie's disappointment of thinking that she was alone, she heard the door open and then the unmistakable clomping of Abby's steal toed shoes against the ceramic tiled floor; darn it she thought, there went her privacy.

Abby was one of the few female technicians belonging to *Aviation World* who repaired heavy aircraft parts. Her steel toed shoes were a requirement. Like the men, Abby had short hair, smelled of grease and skydrol and wore a t-shirt with the words *Aviation World* embossed on it; she also wore a heavy blue jeans. The only signs of her being of the female gender were of a short stature, full lips and big boobs. Many times Nelly was asked if her friend Abby was gay; from Nelly that answer was a big "heck no and none of your business anyway." Abby was outspoken with men, wanted them to accept her as one of them, and, yet in contrast, was looking for one of them to replace her deceased husband. She was a widow and she was looking for someone that saw her for herself, just like her late husband did. He saw past the women who had to make it in a man's world to the loving woman beneath that made the perfect wife.

"Oh lord, it smells in here," Abby spoke as she crinkled up her nose.

With embarrassment in her voice Nelly hollered back through the stall as she reached down and picked up the Lysol spray from the floor, "Well I didn't come in here to bake a cake."

"Geeze," Abby was even more disgusted after Nelly sprayed; "now it smells like someone shit flowers." Abby leaned over to look under the stall to make sure that it was Nelly she was criticizing. She thought that she recognized Nelly's black flats and the bottom of her green leisure suit.

"Nelly, is that you?" she asked.

Nelly didn't answer so Abby continued on by using the orange gritty scrub to get the grease from her hands and then rinsed them off. Then she pulled a paper towel out of the dispenser and wiped her hands dry. There was some "frew-frew" lotion, as everyone in the company liked to call it, on the sink and Abby used it to help relieve the dry cracks in her hands.

This was another first for Nelly in her eternal endeavor to portray the image of a perfect lady; first she cussed at her boss and now she was caught stinking up the bathroom. Nelly grabbed some toilet paper and wiped away her tears, now flowing freely down her full cheeks. The gig was up; Abby knew it was her in the stall so there was no need in hanging in there until she heard the door close.

Just then, Abby heard Nelly sniff and guessed that Nelly was crying.

"I'm sorry Nelly, It doesn't stink that badly," Abby sincerely apologized thinking that she had truly upset Nelly with her connotations concerning the stench; curiously, Nelly wasn't usually that sensitive. They went on at each other all the time.

In the words describing a crying child, Nelly was "supped—supping" or still sniffling as she came out of the stall, "It's not you Abby, I just came from Adam's office and he wants to move me. 'I responded by making a fool out of myself and told him I had to take a "shit."

"No way, you didn't!" Abby said as her large grey eyes sparkled with humor.

"What did he say to that?" she laughed.

"I didn't give him time. I just ran."

"No way!" Abby repeated her explication.

Then she apologized, "I'm sorry, but that's just plain funny."

Nelly ignored Abby's last statement, "I really should quit but it will mean I have to move to Memphis and I hate Memphis, I'm scared of the crime. 'Also, my husband will have to put up with me twenty-four hours a day and you know how that will turn out."

Abby knew what she was talking about because she had heard them arguing many times over the phone. Nelly appeared to take a lot of lecturing under the pretense of her husband's claim to the right to express himself. It often seemed that the only one expressing himself was him; but then there were always two sides to every story. Nelly was hard to get to know but once you did, her personality generally grew on you and you were better off. Just the same, Abby Winters imagined that Nellie McMillan's constant fretting and eye for detail probably drove her husband crazy; no one sees their own faults.

Abby looked helplessly at Nelly and decided to take control of the situation before Nelly started fretting, "Suck it up old girl, we've got work to do. 'Everybody suffers here; we technicians make way below industry standards.' If it was up to me, I'd do things a lot differently, but it's not."

Having suddenly lost her husband just a few years ago to a heart attack, Abby had little tolerance for people who felt sorry for themselves. Nelly appreciated this trait in Abby. Abby was a strong women who often could turn a man's, or woman's, nature against themselves. Abby didn't like drama; all she wanted was to wisely take the advantage of enjoying what God given life she had been given while on this earth.

Nelly grinned and in her best English accent proclaimed, "Stiff upper lip and all that rot, you know."

Abby thought that Nelly's accent wasn't bad, but for a mid-westerner, not an Englishwomen. Nelly was originally from somewhere up north before she met and married her husband at the tender age of eighteen. Being nearly fifty, she was now the new thirty and looked every bit in her thirties.

Nelly washed her face and pulled her make-up case out of her designated plastic bin. Looking into the mirror she applied some peach lipstick and then put her make-up case back before heading back out into the vestibule—with Abby tailing behind her.

From the vestibule, Nelly and Abby heard the sound of a commotion coming from the area of the cubicles. Abby gave Nelly a quizzical and puzzled look.

"What's going on do you suppose," Abby asked more rhetorical than a question.

"I don't know. 'It sounds like it's coming from my cube."

The cubicles were just that, four dark grey cubes, two on each side with a small walkway between them. Model helicopters and airplanes peaked over the top of each cubical wall. A big clock with a picture of a MD 88 was the only wall decoration. As they followed the sound of the commotion, which now sounded like it was coming from the cubicle next to Nelly's, they were able to discern the sound of the voice of Nelly's cube mate, Tracy.

As they rounded the corner, Adam was standing outside Tracy's cube coxing her to let go of Heather, one of the young warehouse employees. Adam was blocking the door as if Tracy was a caged animal about to escape and he was the zoo keeper keeping a wild animal contained.

"She was trying to steal my pocket book!" Tracy furious voice carried over the top of the cubes to Nelly's and Abby's ears, as she was bent on saving her most precious possession. "She's a thief, she's trying to steal my pocket book; can't you see what she is doing?" Tracy was tall and voluptuous in a girlish, hour—glass way. She worked out at her dojo religiously, which was at least four times a week, and at the age of forty-eight had a hard body that looked better than most twenty year olds.

Adam said seriously, "Tracy let her go,—under no circumstances do we condone work place violence here…. if you don't let her go I will fire you."

"I suppose you condone thievery? I caught her putting all my things in a box…not to mention my purse. Fire her for stealing." Tracy's voice still sounded high and argumentative as she put the emphases on the word her.

Abby and Nelly looked at each other and grinned. This turn of events added to Nelly's situation of a series of unfortunate events which now casted a new light on their once beloved boss as being the villain in this scenario—it all seemed like a surreal soap opera.

"This I have to see," Nelly said as she hurried down the small hall with Abby still in tow. When the two of them reach the opening to Tracy's cube, Nelly and Abby pushed Adam aside and peaked in like two little girls impishly peaking through the door of a circus tent for a free show. The site was of Tracy holding a blond headed Heather, looking like a beauty queen—in a martial arts arm bar. Tracy was just doing what seemed natural to protect her things, things were important to Tracy. Her Ex-husband took things away from her and she hated her things taken away from her, but she still loved her Ex-husband.

"Dang, Abby," Nelly said at an attempt at humor, hoping to defuse the situation, "You don't see that every day."

"What's that" Abby jumped into the banter as she leaned back cockily on one hip and crossed her arms.

"Tracy has a hold on Heather!"

It seemed so unnatural to see Tracy looking sporty in her blue silk blouse, pencil style navy skirt and two inch heals straining with all her strength to hold Heather flat faced down in an "arm bar" against cold grey surface of her desk. Tracy's face was red with anger as she was bent on performing the restraining of what she considered a thief. Tracy was always dressed perfectly with well styled hair and matching accessories. Tracy was so obsessed with appearances that once she became upset and wanted to go home to change because, she felt that she created a fashion "fopaux" by wearing black pants with a navy blue blouse. However, she still looked fabulous, she always looked fabulous. Personally, Nelly saw a fashion "fopaux" as wearing one pink sock with one yellow sock at the same time, which she had once managed to accomplish one mind-fogy morning.

"Hey Tracy, the quarters of a cube are a little tight for a girl fight. Why don't you bring it out in the hall," Nelly suggested with one side of her lip turned up in a half grin.

"Adam go get the guys together, they should enjoy this." The guys meant about twenty-five technicians in the shops and they all had the kind humor which would allow them to watch a girl fight with complete enjoyment and without interference. They may even venture on taking bets as to who would win.

Nelly had an unusual way of defusing situations with her dry sense of humor and sarcasm; if you didn't know Nelly it might offend you. However, Tracy knew Nelly, and knew that she wouldn't make light of the situation unless it was for her own protection and it seemed to bring Tracy to her senses. Tracy let go of Heather; then smoothed and straightened her skirt as if she was catching her breath before she had to explain. Meanwhile, Heather rubbed her arm and then her face to stimulate the circulation.

Then Tracy pointed an accusing finger at Heather. "She had a box and was stealing all my things," Tracy explained in frustration as she addressed Nelly instead of Adam this time. Tracy seemed to be calming down from her anger and was grasping at straws toward explaining her insane action of restraining Heather; meanwhile, in turn, searching everyone's face to make some sense out of the insane actions of Heather.

Nellie poked Adam with her elbow to encourage him to take the lead. When he didn't take the lead, Nelly iterated in her best animated southern drawl that mimicked what was typically known in the south as the quick wit of an old southern gentleman, "Boy, I believe that the miss-func-tion-ality that we have here is a complete lack of com-mun-i-ca-tion." Nelly was known for her unique ability to mimic voices in a way that could bring characters to life and a smile to the lips of even the poorest soul.

Then Nellie's tone of voice went more serious as she pressed on, "Well, go ahead and explain it to Tracy,—hell, explain it to me."

The now free, Heather took the opportunity to squeeze her young slender body past the ladies and pointed a finger in Adam's face, "If you don't take action for work place violence against Tracy, I will."

Being Tracy's best friend, helped stirred Abby's maternal instincts and a red faced Abby started after the blond bombshell. Sequentially, Nelly reached out and grabbed Abby's t-shirt causing Abby to spring back, all the while still addressing Adam.

"So tell Tracy what this is all about, Adam," Nellie looked at Adam with anticipation. How would he explain himself with no fancy office and without lording over her by making her wait for thirty minutes?

He was getting furious over the blatant disrespect he was receiving and really didn't know how to approach this situation.

Nelly continued before Adam could speak, "Mr. Wooddale is moving us out to the warehouse and replacing us with the younger models, with less experience."

"Heather was just following orders and moving your stuff, right Adam?" Abby guessed as she jumped in while waiting for Adam's answer; meanwhile, Adam became more irritated.

Then Abby looked up at Adam again and asked without regard to her own position, "Isn't that what age discrimination is all about?"

It was then that Abby realized that she was being over confident and probably pushed too far. The veins on Adam's neck stood out so obviously that she thought that they would burst, spewing red sticky blood all over the cube. She could almost imaging steam physically coming out of his ears.

"This has gotten out of hand, the three of you get your things and get out!" he yelled angrily. Then stopping to think about his actions for a minute he added, "You three are being suspended for insubordination without pay for two weeks…that should give you enough time to appreciate having a job." He swung around and walked off.

"What now," Abby said frustrated at being a part of something for which, in the beginning, she had no part.

Soon after that, Steve rounded the corner. "Adam said to watch you three and escort you out of the building. What's going on?"

"We're being suspended for fighting," now Abby was upset and on the verge of tears. She couldn't figure how the turn of events resulted in her being suspended too. All she did was to run into Nelly in the bathroom.

"For what? 'For fighting?!" He started to howl with laughter as he asked in disbelief. He stopped laughing upon a threatening look from Abby. "OOOps!"

"You coppers get away… we'll go willingly, see" Nellie teased with a nasal sound to her voice.

"Go get your things, ladies, and meet me outside…dinner at *Chic-fil-A* is on me," Tracy promised. Tracy was suddenly scarred that it was all her fault that her friends were in trouble and she somehow wanted to make it up to them by buying dinner. Also, Tracy thought that meeting for dinner would give them time to discuss what just happened before going home…they needed time in which to vent. This way they all wouldn't be going home to their perspective empty houses to have their individual perspective nervous breakdowns; nervous breakdowns preformed in the company of others were much more controlled and safer.

Being a widow, Abby's only companion was an Urn of ashes that she carried around in her truck, Nellie's husband commuted from his job in Tennessee and Tracy was divorced. That made their houses empty.

Tracy had mistakenly left her husband in hopes that the act of a separation would shake up their relationship so that they would reconnect again; instead he immediately divorced her. She had no intention of divorcing and still, after years, she harbored a deep affection for her Ex-husband. She missed him tremendously and compared all who she dated with him. She was also worried about what would happen to her if she lost her job and had no husband in which to depend.

It wasn't possible for Steve to watch all three of them at the same time so he suggested that Abby go back to the shop to pick up her stuff while he stayed with Nelly and Tracy. He knew that the three women didn't see him as anything other than a fun guy to distract them from the perils of a harsh job, so he wondered if they would take him seriously as a security escort. In reality, at age forty-five, he probably was the most eligible bachelor in the building. He was smart, muscular and good looking; so much so that he also had to protect his privacy from the women who were after him, or so he thought. They tried to guess whether he shaved his head because he was balding or whether he just liked the shaved look. However, the shaved head didn't distract from his muscular physic, his big green eyes or the dimples in each cheek.

Nelly accomplished gathering her things first. She was fast at everything she did and, after giving Steve her security badge, went out the front door without waiting for the others. She decided she needed space and would wait outside on the front sidewalk. A least it was a clear day, she thought as she stood looking down the sidewalk at a row of perfectly groomed hedges planted in a bed of pine chips slightly chartreuse in color. She was a little shaken concerning the turn of events and had an appetite for pure chocolate instead of a *"Chic-fil-A."* Being suspended was definitely hard on a gal's emotions, she sentimentally thought in the verbiage of her dead mid-western father. He used the words "hard on a guy" or "gal" when occasions such as this arose.

    She walked over to her Chrysler P.T. Cruiser convertible and put her things in the back. They were heavy and she didn't want to stand on the sidewalk any longer. As she flopped into the front seat, she turned the car on and wound the top down. While listening to high pitched whining sound of the motor automatically pulling the top down, she noticed the big print Bible that she took everywhere with her sitting on the passenger seat and it reminded her to say a little prayer to get them through this ordeal. She also prayed that God would reveal the reason this happened. She put the Bible into the glove department and, once the top was down, she turned off the car and waited. Nelly pulled her blue jacket from the backseat and put it on the floor under the passenger seat. She thought with the top down it might get cool enough for a jacket and she wanted it close. She thought again that she would love to have a big box of Whitman's chocolate right now as chocolate always help her feelings.

    Shrugging that thought off, Nelly picked up her other favorite book, *"The Complete Instruction Bible for Data Bases,"* from the driver's door pocket and started reading it to preoccupy her time while she waited. She was trying to pick up a few more tricks toward applying easy search functions for collating information all in one place.

    When Abby came out of the building, she saw Nelly sitting in the Cruiser, put her things in her white diesel extend-a-cab truck and went to sit with Nelly while they waited for Tracy. Tracy would take more time because Tracy was one of those types of women who liked her stuff and had a lot of it, even at work—it was like a girl scout in that she wanted to "always be prepared" for every occasion—she had stashes like Pain Relievers for a headaches and tablets for gastroenteritis. Amongst other things she carried a sewing kit, peanuts or almonds for a quick snack and extra pantyhose for runs. One could always count on Tracy to have what was needed in an emergency.

Abby smiled and teased Nelly about her book concerning data bases, "Ummm that looks interesting; if I read that, I'd get a good night's sleep."

Nelly didn't ignore her on purpose but had the natural gift of tuning people out.

Then Abby, looking thoughtful, said as she crawled into the passenger seat, "I was thinking that I don't really want a Chic-filet that much. I would much rather go to *McMulligan's* on *Virginia Avenue* for a drink. They have the best Rueben sandwiches, which you love, and Salads for Tracy." Tracy always ate salads.

"That would be OK with me if it's OK with Tracy," Nelly said as she looked at her watch and put her book back in the door pocket. It was nearly one o'clock and, not having had lunch, she could easily replace her craving for Chocolate with a Rueben."

"OK, let's all go sit down at the bar and talk while I drink myself into a stupor," Abby meant it more as a guffaw than an actuality.

"Good idea," Nelly said with a smile, "let's all go sit at the bar and watch you drink yourself into a stupor." Then she became sidetracked with her own impatience and said, "I'm going back in to see if I can help Tracy. 'She sure is taking her time."

Nelly met Tracy and Steve in the lobby. Both had several boxes filled with dishes, flowers, cheese crackers, thermoses and other things that Tracy felt necessary to survive in office habitat environmental conditions.

Nelly silently took one of the boxes from Tracy and then continued out the front door to Tracy's red jeep, which was right next to the P.T. Cruiser. Tracy balanced her box on one raised knee while opening the tail section so everyone could deposit their load. There wasn't enough room so Tracy opened the passenger door for Steve to put his load in the back seat.

As Steve bent over to put the box in the back seat, the lady's all in unison couldn't help but take a peek at his magnificent backside. He definitely worked out frequently, or nature was good to him. Even his low husky voice sounded muscle bound. Unknowingly, he emitted pheromones through his ears.

Abby, being the most daring upon these occasions coaxed Steve to lean over again by saying, "Did something drop behind the seat over there."

They all gave each other a knowing grin and continued to enjoy the view one more time as he looked on the floor board.

"No, I don't see anything." He said in ignorance of Abby's intent.

Then all in unison the women said, "Thanks."

Steve suspected that they were up to something but didn't quite get it. He straightened up and said, "Your welcome," then he said uncomfortably, "I'll be going back now."

The ladies all starred at him as if they all were on a hunger strike and he was a piece of steak. He didn't know whether to be flattered or offended. Nelly snapped out of it first and turned red. These days Nelly spent most of her life in a state of self discipline buried in a computer program book, essentially ignoring that she had any sexual attraction for the opposite sex. She had her reasons for behaving this way and did it on purpose. Also, a contributing factor was that Nelly didn't see herself as desirable. Over the years she spent too much time scrubbing the proverbial toilet and hunting practical clothes for her family. On the other hand, Tracy and Abby were in touch with their sensuality and gravitated toward desires; seeing them as perfectly natural.

Tracy did have one serious relationship a year after her divorce; it was with a younger man. He hurt her badly when he told her that she was too old for him. However, in reality Tracy at Forty-eight was so much more active than her younger boyfriend and also looked so much younger. It was unfair to break up based on age and it nearly crushed her.

"OK, thanks again," Nelly interjected embarrassed at getting caught admiring Steve's backside.

Steve thought that once Nelly would have been strikingly beautiful in her younger years. She had a lion's head of ash brown hair streaked with dark brown streaks, big ice blue eyes; a tiny nose and hart shape lips. Although older, she was still beautiful. He had been asked by many a new guy seeking employment if she was single. Hell, if she was ten years younger, he himself probably wouldn't even care if she was married. Right now she was a little older than what he wanted to experience in a woman; but, he was glad to call her a friend.

After Steve was gone, Abby turned to Tracy and told her of the plan to go to *McMulligan's Bar and Grill* instead of *Chic-fil-A*. Tracy took a little convincing but eventually gave in once they all said that they would go Dutch.

Chic-fil-A was a time honored popular southern sandwich and it was a southern tradition for a true southern woman to patronize the faculties of the infamous Chic-filet. It had started as a tiny grill that looked like the Waffle House located in the small town of Hapeville near the Atlanta Airport and then it grew in popularity. Before its beginnings no one had ever heard of filleting a chicken breast, frying it up and putting it on a bun with pickles. Years later *Chic-fil-A's* were in every town and Truett Cathy, the founder, being famous locally, begin adding restaurants like Truett's grill in Morrow, Georgia; which was surrounded outside by his collection of antique cars and filled inside with his collection of antique bikes, wagons and electric trains. His picture was on the wall of most restaurants. He was a local hero in Jonesboro, Georgia, basically because he coined the phrase "rags to riches." He was honest and gave back to society too, like hiring college students and giving them scholarships.

However, *McMulligan's* sounded like it was more befitting for of the occasion of being put on suspension for two weeks.

"Hop in and we'll take my car," Nelly said as she again slid back into the driver's seat. Tracy squeezed into the theater style back seat. Not an easy feat in a tight skirt. The Cruiser was gold with a slightly darker cloth top. Nelly liked the retro look, the versatility, the many hidden compartments and the roominess of a P.T. Cruiser, so she bought it. The seats were of tan leather and the dash was designed fashionably with the wood look.

After they left the building, gossip went through the company like a wild fire. No one could believe the two office ladies and the happy-go-lucky female technician were suspended for fighting. The story became embellished and soon the lady's were all rolling on the lobby floor fighting with Adam in a free for all.

CHAPTER 4

Drowning Our Sorrows

By the time the three of them rolled into *McMulligan's Bar and Grill's* parking lot, even thought it was just fifteen minutes away from where they worked, the time was two o'clock in the afternoon. It took more time to go back and wait for Tracy to hunt for her sun glasses in the mound of boxes taken out to her car and for Abby brazenly to go down in the woods past the Bradford Pairs to take a "piss." Nelly teased that Abby had to hike her leg upon the property and like a dog showing attitude.

"I piss in your general direction," Nelly said mimicking a terrible French accent as she drove again out of *Aviation World's* parking lot; meanwhile, gesturing by flipping out her hand from under her chin.

"Where do you get this stuff," Abby asked with a snicker.

"I call them un-quotes because I really don't know; they are similar to things I've heard before but not really what I heard if that make sense," Nelly laughed, "I make things up as I go—I make up my own words to songs too."

It was a typical Thursday afternoon for the restaurant bar; which meant that it was completely empty. The bar was located in the middle of

McMulligan's Bar and Grill restaurant on a raised floor surrounded by uncomfortable wooden chair-backed stools. As they walked into restaurant, Nelly noticed that the whole building was lined with charming windows that allowed a view of the airport runway, it was designed for attracting customers who enjoyed watching commercial jets as they hurled down the runway and launched into the air. Business men sitting at scattered tables seemed to be the predominant cliental. Nelly expected that they were either staying across the street at *The Luxurious Hillcrest Grand Garden Inn* or that they came from one or the other nearby general office complexes. *The Luxurious* Hillcrest Grand *Garden Inn* attracted weekly sales conventions and other business type meetings typical for large companies. Nelly had never been inside the *Hillcrest* but was told that it was eloquent in a utilitarian way. It had restaurants, shops and bars.

As the women each crawled up on a wooden bar stool, Nelly immediately enjoyed the atmosphere of old-fashioned Midwestern décor. The theme was of wood and leather; the inset lighting created a soft golden glow. At one end of the bar, lattice style racks held bottles of liquor and wine in neat rows; and just a few feet above them, wine glasses hung by their stems. Bowls of peanuts lined the cozy U-shaped bar which served least fifteen people on each side. Bar's were a new experience for Nelly and she already liked them; they reeked of friendliness.

Abby picked up a peanut from a bowl on the counter and threw it at Nelly while saying, "Smile and relax."

Abby seemed aware of the constant battle between Nelly's inner Church Lady and her fun loving inner party girl. Then again, Abby guessed that Nelly may have had deeper reasons for her heightened sense of discipline. She once heard a fleeting story that indicated Nelly's Mom was once a party girl. She wondered, could those memories be putting a dampener on Nelly's ability to let her hair down?

"Ok," she smiled, "but I'm not going to drink."

Abby looked irritated, "Nobody is going to make you drink, you old fool."

Just then a tall thin bar tender with the big toothy grin of a man wanting big tips used his naturally friendly nature to ask for their names. After writing their names down on a seating chart, the bar tender took their drink orders and gave them a menu.

Abby ordered a bottle of their best beer and Tracy ordered a white zinfandel, while Nelly ordered a tomato juice with a lemon twist. Tomato juice with a twist was always a less noticeable method, both visually and verbally, when it came to the subterfuge of not drinking alcohol. Tomato juice looked like a mixed drink and verbally ordering "a twist" flowed like a professional drinker.

Abby asked Nelly, "Where did you get the name Nelly anyway?" 'It doesn't fit you; you're such a tiny little thing."

She seemed genuinely curious and Nelly never minded talking about herself to someone who was interested in listening.

"My name comes from a family name passed on from one generation to the next. 'It's actually Petronelli but shortened to Nelly, " Nelly explained

Nelly continued on, anticipating what Abby would say next, "I know… I know it sounds kind of like I'm the family's old mule called Nelly. *'Whoa Nelly not so fast there in plowing that filed* sounds more natural to a sentence with the name Nelly… right? 'I always wanted to be a Selena, a Sofia or even an Amanda, anything but Nelly"

"What is your middle name?"

"My Name is Petronelli Anastasia Bultsa McMillan."

"From now on we dub you Annie and from this day forth we will call you by your true name," she teased.

Nelly turned up her nose to that name too.

"At least they didn't shorten it to Petro or Peter," Nelly sounded grateful.

They both snickered at those names.

Tracy couldn't believe Nelly's and Abby's light heartedness in times of serious peril and she reminded them of it. "So what do we do now that we are out of work for two weeks?" she asked. She couldn't believe that the two of them were concentrating on something as trivial as Nelly's name when they should be planning a counter action to being almost fired.

Abby thought for a second and then said, "Why don't we drive down to Florida?"

"With what money, remember we're not being paid for two weeks," Tracy said in disbelief.

Tracy had the knack for looking at things pessimistically but Abby shot that down by saying, "With my money. 'My husband left me some money and a pension—and I have my own retirement checks from the service, luckily I started young and retired young. 'The money I earned at Aviation World is just extra."

Nelly knew how much Abby missed Joe by looking at the pain in Abby's eyes when she mentioned his name. Nelly's heart went out to Abby. Joe was good to Abby and good men were hard to find. Abby was a housewife for many years and only took up her earlier habits as a technician in the army to work for *Aviation World* merely to get her mind off of him. She really didn't have to work; Joe took care of her both in life, as well as death.

"I can provide the transportation," Nelly jumped in the conversation excitedly in order to change the subject.

Then she said in a huff, "No, that wouldn't work,—I'd have to explain this all to my husband and he is going to be upset enough as it is."

Just then, four work weary looking gentlemen sat down at the bar directly opposite and ordered drinks. After setting the men up with drinks, the bartender took the ladies lunch order. Abby, still in a rare generous mood, sent another round of drinks to the men across the bar, which raised their glasses up in a salute of thanks.

As predicted Tracy ordered a grill chicken salad and Nellie ordered a Rueben on marble bread, but unpredictably Abby ordered a steak and blackened tilapia on a plank. Along with their food another round of drinks showed up and the bar tender volunteered that it was from the gentlemen across the bar. Abby saluted with her beer in the same tradition as they had saluted her. Tracy ducked her head and acted as if she didn't want to encourage them; meanwhile, Nelly blushed, drank her tomato juice and wiped the grease coming from the toasted Rubin off her hands and mouth onto a linen napkin. Her stomach was full after eating only a half her sandwich so she asked for a box for the other half and sat it on the bar.

Soon the drinks started to lighten the mood of Tracy as she had another, and then another.

Then feeling pretty good, Tracy ordered a long island tea. Abby ordered an Irish Car Boom and tried to talk Nelly into guzzling one down with her. Nelly stuck to her guns but was having a pretty good time laughing with the two of them without being in an inebriated state of mind. The men across the bar were really getting into the fun of the three women giggling like school girls so they sent another round. You don't often see three women who looked like soccer moms enjoying a drink where the business community usually haunts.

Then, after the empty plates were cleared away, the four men moved from one side of the bar to the other and struck up a conversation with the women. Nelly, who was not used to the attention, tentatively led in a friendly chat by asking questions in order to encouraging the men into monopolize the conversation. It seemed that all three of them worked for *The Atlanta Computer Corporation*, or otherwise described as A.C.C., as representatives consulting with *Low-Fare Airlines* on a new work process review of the airline's computer systems. The airline was led the market of saving money for their customers and many of the other airlines followed suit.

Low-Fare Airlines put them up at the *Hillcrest Grand Garden Inn* for a couple of days to lecture on the use of a program that tracked the life limits on installed aircraft parts through radio bar code scanners. Apparently the industry had finally developed a ceramic barcode plate lightweight enough to attach to engine parts but strong enough to take the extreme heat. Also, Nelly found out that two of them were happily married, one of them was just barely the legal age of twenty-one, while the other was a single guy who owned his own computer consultant firm; he was the consultant for the consultants of A.C.C. Apparently John, the consultant of the consultants, was doing the physical work of setting up wireless systems in the technical operations base.

The afternoon rolled on in fun and conversation until Tracy broke things up, having drunk too much to know what she was doing she proceeded to break up the group by asking, "Ladies, you know what we need?"

Abby slurred her words as she said, "No, but I'm sure you're about to tell us."

Tracy waved her hand out of control and picked up a peanut. She pulled a marker out of her purse and drew a face on one end of the peanut and started talking in a little girl voice as if the peanut was a puppet.

"We all need sex!!! 'That's what we need!!" she said while bouncing the peanut around.

Abby burst into a belly laugh and, while the gentlemen also laughed whole heartedly, the married men started to make their drunken excuses and the young one agreed.

"I'm too drunk," one laughed.

Nelly made excuses for Tracy, "She wouldn't say that unless she had too much to drink, anyway she means it in a sense of stress relieving generalities and not as proposition to you *fine* gentlemen."

Tracy slurred out more words but this time to Nelly, "That's right and thank you Nelly."

"Too bad," the married bald headed man said jovially but looked relieved, it was a good save. He already felt guilty that he was sitting here having fun with three attractive women while his wife was sitting at home with the children.

Nelly was sitting on the stool next to the business owner who was the consultant for the consultant of the consultant and his attention turned to Nelly.

"Little lady, I just noticed you're not drinking," he said and then asked "do you ever?"

That was a one word answer.

"No."

My name is John, what is yours," he asked

"Nelly, and you'll have to forgive us, we aren't like this normally. 'We've had an extremely bad morning at work that resulted in all three of us being suspended," She went on to tell him the rest of the story.

"Hell, well, it sounds to me like you all have the unusual opportunity to embark upon an adventure, like a nice vacation. 'Why don't *ya'll* go down to Florida and, if you want to, you can drive over to *"Biloxi, Mississippi"* on Monday and spend a couple of days with me. 'I'm renting some of rooms on a business discount for my employees at the *Belle Rose Casino* on the Gulf and *ya'll* can have one of the rooms for yourselves. 'No pressure, this is not a proposition or anything, we're not a bunch of dirty old men, and I just thought you all'd be a bunch of fun. 'I'll tell you what; I'll even teach you how to gamble—hell, go have fun, life is too short." He slapped a meaty hand on the bar like it was a judge's gavel finalizing his official verdict.

"Abby just suggested that," she volunteered as she thought of the tempting proposition. She heard that the *Belle Rose Casino* was a beautiful upscale hotel. It was luxurious and anyone who stayed there felt spoiled.

"I don't think so, but thank you anyway, kind sir," Nelly smiled back at him, and then looked at the other two women to see if they had heard any of the conversation. They hadn't.

He grabbed little wireless cell phone off of the bar and typed his number into her contacts.

"If you change your mind, my number is in your cell."

They talked on exclusively for awhile until he got up, looked at his watch, and said, "Well, it's late and I've had too much to drunk. 'I have meeting at eight P.M tonight and that's just an hour from now, so I better get sobered up and get my wits about me. "

Nelly couldn't believe that they all had been sitting there for nearly five hours. She thought the bar tender must be happy because she knew Abby had probably dropped nearly three-hundred dollars and the business men twice that much.

"Nice to meet you, Ms Nelly," John said as he stood up and caught his balance, "I don't know when I've had this much fun." Then as an afterthought, "Think about it."

She watched John as he walked away. He was tall and big but solid, like a football player. His hair was extremely thick with blondish, reddish tints and graying at the temples. He said that he was fifty-eight years old and, although his skin looked as though it had seen some outdoor living, he was ruggedly handsome. Denying her own attraction to him, she thought there could be a possibility to match him up with one of the other two, but they were too uncharacteristically drunk to discuss it right now.

The other men made their excuses and thanked the ladies before staggering back to the hotel to sleep it off. The young one tipped his baseball cap and said, "Nighty, nite, Ladies."

"One thing I'd like to say about *McMulligan's* is what happens at *McMulligan's* stays at *McMulligan's*, just like *Los Vegas*—usually only out of town business men patronize the restaurant's bar and I don't want any of this to get around at work," Tracy threatened the other two women and put her arm around their shoulders to steady herself. It was nice to step out of your role as a lady once in awhile, Nelly thought.

Nelly remembered a story that her mother-in-law told her once. As a little girl of eight in the depression years of the 1930s, little Janice was swinging on a make shift swing in the back yard singing "I'm a look'n for the local bully…" over and over again. Her mother scolded her saying,

"Now Janice that doesn't sound like a lady." And now, to this day, at ninety years old Janice McMillan still feels the disappointment of having to stop her fun. "I was so disappointed." she'd say, "because I was having sooo much fun." Nelly loved that story. Nelly loved her mother-in-law and all the cute stories that she told.

"Amen," Abby made an attempt at agreeing with Tracy's idea of keeping it in the group.

"Hey, they didn't give us their names," Abby said as she thought about it.
"I guess, why should they"

"You know, this was deliciously naughty as I didn't know hanging out at a bar all afternoon could be so much fun, we need to do it again sometime, it's a good stress relief," Nelly giggled as she expressed her concluding argument for justifying enjoying herself.

"Yeah, but leave out the part where we get suspended from work…off," Abby said as she stumbled over the words.

"You are such a nerd, Nelly," Tracy responded to Nelly's earlier statement as she hugged Nelly playfully.

The bar tender gave Abby and Tracy a bottle of water but it was too late, they were already too far gone. Abby worried how she was going to get them to the car when, to her relief, Steve came into the bar and sat down beside them. It seemed that he was worried about the ladies and, having overheard that they were going to *McMulligan's Bar and Grill*, and seeing their cars still in the parking lot, he decide to check on them.

He was glad to find them still there but Nelly was happier to see him. The other two ladies were too snookered to attempt walking to the car completely on their own so Nelly desperately needed Steve's assistance in walking them out as normally as possible without drawing attention. She wanted to keep everyone's dignity intact, as they would do it for her if the situation was reversed. Nelly and Steve managed to guide Abby and Tracy out of the restaurant and tuck them in the back seat of the Cruiser. Nelly threw the box with the other half of her sandwich in the passenger seat in hopes that it wouldn't spoil.

"I took the day off tomorrow if you need anything," Steve offered as he shyly looked to the right across the parking lot. "I just needed a day off."

Nelly naively missed Steve's invitation to spend the day with him; a frustrated Steve thought that he could stand there naked with a rose in his teeth and she still wouldn't get the hint. She surely didn't mind joking and teasing him at work but, by her response, he realized that it was just a platonic game for her. Instead she was busy apologizing for taking up his time and indicating relief at the same time that he chose to check up on them. She asked Steve to go with her while she took everyone home and suggested that she could bring him back to pick up his car later that night if he would moved it back to the work parking lot for safety. He jumped at the chance.

"If you could please just help me take them home, I would appreciate it. I believe that they are too messed up to make it on their own," she explained.

Just then Abby stuck her head out the side window and laughed, "Hey Steve, I'll show you mine if you show me yours." Then she started to do her version of a drunken cackle.

"I see what you mean," Steve said pretending to be disgusted.

CHAPTER 5

Detour on the Road Home

After dropping off Steve's car, they drove south on I-85 toward Tracy's house in Fairburn. Guessing that Steve hadn't eaten, Nelly offered him her left over Rubin. As Steve gobbled down Nelly's left over sandwich, Nelly and Steve rehashed what happened at *Aviation World* that morning. They were so deep in conversation that Nelly didn't notice that she had completely driven past the exit and was miles down the road.

"Damn, I missed the exit…now we have back track," she cussed.

"Why not just keep going?" Steve suggested whole heartedly.

Nelly checked Steve's expression to see if he was serious. While she thought over Steve's suggestion, Nelly decided to put the top up so that the sleeping ladies in the back seat wouldn't be exposed to the cool night air. Abby and Tracy had fallen asleep before they left the parking lot at *McMulligan's* and were too oblivious to the shenanigans that Steve and Nelly were about to embark upon.

She nodded her head toward the backseat, "You're the third person that has suggested that today. 'If I went to Florida without asking them, they will have my hide."

"I'll wake them up and ask," Steve grinned slyly and reached back to shake both of their knees.

"Hey, do you two want to go to Florida?" Steve asked in his deep voice.

In a sleepy haze both, not fully in a comprehensive state of mind, said, "Yeah sure."

"See," he said, "there you go!"

"They don't know what they're saying, they are both a little confused and disoriented right now," Nelly hedged but really wanted to go through with it.

"Well?" Steve prompted.

"We've… well I've…. never done anything like this before," Nelly said suddenly embarrassed at the day's events, "It's like it's not us, or me, to which all this has happened. 'It's like another person."

Steve thought her embarrassment as kind of innocent and charming.

Just then Nelly's cell phone rang with the sound of the theme to a Cartoon Tune. As Nelly warned him that it was David calling, Steve tensed up in his seat at the sound of David's name. He didn't quite know what to do, the devil in him wanted his voice to carry across the phone just to irritate David …but then again her husband may get the wrong idea…or right idea…Steve didn't know what he was doing her either.

"Where are you?" David sounded upset, "Neal called and said that you didn't come home. 'It's nine o'clock at night; surely you're still not at work."

Neal was their twenty-five year old son who still lived with Nelly in their Atlanta home. Neal's sister, Julia, their other child, lived near Nashville, Tennessee just three and a half hours from Memphis. The living arrangements were odd as the whole family lived all over the country, even the parents were separated by distance. If it wasn't for access to modern day transportation, the weekly commutes for family time would have been impossible.

Nelly did feel a little guilty at what she planned to do without David's permission and was tempted to turn back; however, temptation toward the road called her so instead she proclaimed as innocently as possible, "I'm headed to Florida with the women's group from work." They had all been out together and gone off on weekends excursions before so she called them "the women's group from work" just like she called her church group "the women's group from church." Nelly had different groups in accordance to the occasion; however, what was different this time was that former trips were well planned and not made on the spur of the moment.

She held the phone away from her ear because now his voice was too loud over the receiver to hold it too close to her eardrum. "What!" He yelled.

"I said that I'm headed to Florida with the women's group at work."

"That's what I thought you said, but what in the hell for. Don't you have to work tomorrow?"

That's right she thought as she cringed, throughout all the chaos she had forgotten to call her husband to explain the circumstances around her new found freedom for two weeks.

"The three of us were put on suspension and so we decided to take off to Florida…that is while we have the time off… actually we decided that just now, as we speak." She purposely left Steve out of the equation for obvious reasons.

Nelly explained the whole suspension to her husband and he seemed to understand, but suggested very strongly that she turn the car around and take her "little friends" home; he talked to her like she was a child and her friends were some stray kitty-cats picked up in a dumpster behind the supermarket—and now it was time to take them to the pound. He had a way of making her and others feel beneath him.

"I know you have a kind heart and you want to console your friends… Nelly… but you need to come to your senses."

Her intention was that she was going to do this regardless, meaning of his approval, but she didn't say that straight out. Instead she said as calmly as she could, "Adam is a good boss and he wouldn't have suspended us if the situation didn't call for it. We probably need the time to think this through. …Good bye David, my cell is fading in a valley—I'll call you later."

Steve eyed Nelly and grinned while saying, "I guess we are going to Florida, aren't we?"

CHAPTER 6

All about David

At the condo in Memphis, David reached over his newest lover, who was sleeping next to him in their king size bed, and hung up the phone. He ran his fingers through his thick black hair and pulled the covers off of his long slender legs to put his boney feet into the thick carpet of their bedroom floor. Even though his name was Irish, his mother was Greek so he had inherited her family's tall slender body, he could easily be mistaken for an old statue of a Greek god. He was one of those lucky middle aged men with plenty of dark hair that never grayed with age. David looked like a retired underwear model for Kelvin Klein. His looks drew plenty of attention from the opposite sex. His looks were his best gift and only talent. It was a blessing that helped him through an easy life; it got him his jobs and popularity.

"Hey, wake up," he said as he shook his latest lover Vanessa Strong. Vanessa was a woman he had picked up at work. They had taken a couple of days off to be together before Nelly came home to Memphis for the weekend. Vanessa knew that David was married but she wanted him anyway. She was twenty-five years younger than David and basically looked like a younger version of Nellie. David was flattered by her youth and couldn't resist her flirtatiousness and sense of style.

"I have to fly to Atlanta," he spoke in a true southern drawl that only a true southern gentleman by birth could master. "I think that Nelly is in trouble." He pulled his pants on and went into the bathroom.

That irritated Vanessa as she thought, why would David care what happens to Nelly? Vanessa thought that they had something between them. Until now, she had never guessed that she was just a fling and he thought of her as pure entertainment. She thought that her youth and vigor would win his affections; that he would eventually give up the old bat and marry her. Around Vanessa, David only referred to Nelly as "the bitch," so what changed?

Regardless of how many women he had in his bed, Nelly was still his one and only true love. He never wanted to lose her and worked hard to keep her tied to him. He used every trick in the book to manipulate her into thinking that he was the perfect husband for her, and it worked for most part. She had a strong sense of conscience and he used that against her. He believed that he had the right because she didn't have enough sense to know that he was the only man that could make her happy, and that they were soul mates. When she wasn't around, he missed her company and the touch of her unusually soft skin. On the other hand, sometimes he didn't think that she missed him. As he glanced at himself in the mirror, he thought that he obviously still has his looks—so that wasn't it.

He never understood why Nelly called him intrusive during one of their arguments—he just wanted what was best for Nelly—she said that she was tired of him ordering her around—or just tired, as in worn out, actually he couldn't remember exactly what she said. What he didn't know was that her free spirited soul could handle the other women in his life but her love of life and love of people made her sick of his constant criticism of things for which he knew nothing. He didn't know what happened to make her lose interest in their marriage but he would give his life to have it all back. He wished it was the way it used to be when they first married, when they were young and naive. He would go after her and make her be his wife again.

Vanessa slipped on her pants and shirt while he was in the bathroom. She guessed right in that this would be the last she heard from David.

Vanessa had to say one last thing to David to appease her hurt and all she could think of was, "David, you're and asshole."

He laughed while she stormed out the door and yelled after her, "Honey, don't be mad, it is what it is."

CHAPTER 7

Back on the Road

Meanwhile back in the Cruiser, Nelly hadn't rolled her window up yet and in an act of freedom, she unclipped her long waist length hair from its tight bun to let it blow loose. She yelped "WHOO-HOO" while streamers of hair blew all over the car and out the window Steve watched in fascination as he had never seen so much hair fly everywhere. She looked like a mermaid princes he once saw in a men's cologne commercial on T.V. Like the commercial, her hair fanned out, surrounding her in long soft tendrils, as if it was floating in slow motion through clear water, and then it sucked straight out the window as if she had quickly flipped a long tail fin to swim away. It was one of those glorious moments for which he felt fortunate to have paid witness and it would forever become a fantastical memory in his mind. She looked years younger and much happier.

Then Nelly pointed to a built in drawer under the passenger seat and asked Steve to put in the disc for a popular country western song called *Redneck Riviera* in the CD player. It was perfect music for her mood. As she sang the words she sang over the word Alabama over the word Florida.

Redneck Riviera

Put on old blue Jeans and an old T-shirt,
Let the wind blow through your hair
Turn the music on, life is fun
Cause we're in this old Chevy Truck, on the run

With Reckless thoughts and reckless dreams
Just trusting our luck to the open road
Leave the city behind
Cause we're sick of the grind
Baby, we going out of town tonight

Put on old blue Jeans and an old T-shirt,
Let the wind blow through your hair
Turn the music up, run away with me
Cause we're in this old Chevy Truck, go'n to the sea

Honey, we'll travel through the country side
To make love under the Florida (Alabama) Sky
Go with me to the big Gulf shore
To smell fresh Ocean Air
Just you and me go'n to the redneck Riviera
Baby, go'n to the redneck Riviera.........

As the song played loudly, she checked in the rear view mirror to make sure that her friends were all right and still sleeping peacefully. She hadn't seen them this peaceful in years. As they drove further way from the city the stars shone brighter and the air was fresher.

Steve saw Nelly's blue jacket sticking out from under the passenger seat and pulled it out to cover up his head so he could sleep without the wind blowing in his face. As Steve drifted, Nelly thought about the events of the day. She could hardly comprehend that she had started out at work this morning and, upon a whim, was now headed to the Gulf coast on I 85. She thought that they would start at *Panama City Beach* and work their way west on I10 to *Biloxi* to take up John's offer, if the others agreed, or should she tell them, she thought. She didn't even know John's last name but still she felt like it would be a great opportunity to stay at the best hotel in Mississippi and learn to gamble.

Steve stirred around Midnight and worried about his cat, "I'll call my Ex-wife in the morning and have her and my daughter go feed it." He then went back to sleep. He had the whole weekend to work out the details concerning what to do about work on Monday. He didn't have two weeks off like the others but he would enjoy the mini-vacation of a weekend.

Nelly hadn't thought about maybe needing things like blood pressure medications or anything life threatening. Nelly kept hers in her purse and so did Tracy and she did know that Abby didn't take any medication but she didn't ask Steve. She shook Steve awake. When one becomes middle aged one thinks of such things, she thought.

"I know that this is a crazy time to think about this but do you take any medication," she asked as she shook Steve's shoulder.

"Why, you into drugs?" he yawned still awake.

"No, I'm serious; I was just worried about arriving at the beach and then having to find a pharmacy."

He sat up and rubbed his eyes, "I take 50 mg of Norvasc for high blood pressure and I didn't forget... I was hijacked!"

"Good," she said, "I take the same medication and you can share mine...I'll go to a pharmacy in *Panama City Beach* and claim I lost my pills so I can have extra....now go back to sleep."

"Oh and you weren't high jacked, it was your idea as well....don't you forget that Mister."

The June night air coming through the windows was cool and refreshing as they lost sight of all signs of civilization. Fresh salty air and a new perspective is what lay ahead, and they all needed it.

They also all needed a fresh change of clothes and a place to sleep for the night. This was really roughing it, she smiled at that thought. How things changed, as roughing it when she was a young "lass" in *Montana* meant sleeping on the cold ground in a sleeping bag near Duck Creek, basically fishing for your next meal. No clothes, no food and at the whim of the road was not really considered roughing it. The only thing she had between her and the homeless shelter now was her and her husband's check card.

CHAPTER 8

Montgomery, Alabama

After three hours on the road Nelly pulled off of the interstate in *Montgomery, Alabama* at an all night Super Store to gas up. Realizing that they were stopping, Abby and Tracy woke up groaning from headaches and back seat stiffness so Nelly thought that she might buy some aspirin; and possible a change of clothes but only after she pumped gas. Abby wondered where they were and Nelly broke the news that she was just three hours from *Panama City Beach*. Abby was as agreeable as one could be with a hangover and drifted back to sleep but Tracy was withdrawn, which showed that she was mad.

"Tracy, you're retired from the Airline and you can fly back for free. We'll simply put you on a plane to Atlanta when we reach *Panama City Beach*... if you want to go," Nelly promised.

"Still, you should have asked, I would never have carted you off somewhere while you were asleep without asking," she lectured.

Nelly shrugged her shoulders and continued out of the car to the gas pump. The station was open and amounted to a small covered lighted area at the end of the Wal-Mart parking lot with four pumps. Nelly slid her bank card in the automatic payment slot and filled the thirsty gas tank up with almost thirteen gallons of regular unleaded gas. She then twisted the hose in the opposite direction to avoid gas from spilling all over her before hanging the nozzle up and then she screwed the cap back on the gas tank.

Both Tracy and Nelly's husband, David, were former employees of the Airlines. When the Airlines went bankrupt, they were both forced into an early retirement. David went to an air freight company as an analyst in their jet base in Memphis and Tracy ended up at the same company where Nelly worked. Although neither knew the other, they both took the same retirement package which included free flying benefits.

"Let's do a little shopping to buy a couple of things while we are here," Nelly said as she turned to the back seat, but the two of them had fallen back to sleep while she was pumping gas.

As Nelly drove closer to Wal-Mart's main entrance, she woke the two sleeping beauties again. Tracy was aghast that Nelly would consider buying Wal-Mart clothes to wear but gave in when she realized that this would be the only place open at one a.m. on a Friday morning. The urge to freshen up drove them out of the backseat of the four door vehicle and into the Wal-Mart ladies room.

At first Tracy looked like she wasn't going to be a sport about all this but calmed down when they entered the store. The restroom was clean enough so Nelly went to the restroom and then, after washing up, pulled her brush out of her purse. While the others cleaned up, she thought that she would fix her hair. Nelly was regretting the consequences of letting her hair blow freely in the wind, she had snarls the size of a birds' nests. She looked like a wild women on a bad day. Before it's all over with she decided that she would cut her hair as she again styled it back into a twist, clamping it with a comb she kept in her purse. Tracy reapplied her lipstick and Abby just turned her head a few times to assess the damage. Abby wasn't much into makeup.

A CHANGE OF LUCK

"Let's all dress up like teenagers for the week," Nelly said in her golly gee wiz I'm so cute voice while making the motion of putting her index finger in a pretend dimpled cheek. Then she skipped out of the bathroom into the store.

"Yeah, we'll wear hip huggers with thong panties hanging out the top," Abby laughed as she waved her hand in a jester that none verbally indicated to Tracy lets all skip out after Nelly.

"I don't believe that the term is hip huggers anymore," Tracy corrected Abby as if she was the old school morm amongst the group.

The store looked abandoned. In Atlanta one could go a Wal-Mart Super Store any time of the day or night and still have to stand in line but apparently not in Alabama.

After Nelly's suggestion, they all suddenly were in good humor again; at one a.m. in the morning still slightly sauced, they bee-lined to the junior section of a strange Wal-Mart, three hours from home no less, looking for children's clothes to wear to the beach. Who would have thought it, Nelly thought but Abby and Tracy was thinking, no way would they ever wear children's clothes.

However, being a sport, Abby pulled a T-shirt from a circular rack of bright pink *Junior Rock Band* inscribed T-shirts with large sparkling red sequent shaped hearts on the front and proclaimed that it would look good on Nelly. Nelly tried to talk the other two into matching T-shirts and low riding blue jeans. However, in the end, Abby went to the men and boys section to buy herself some camouflage fatigues and a billed army cap. While Tracy went to women's, proclaiming under her breath that she wouldn't be caught dead in public wearing children's clothes.

In case they changed their mind, Nelly picked out three of the matching t-shirts and herself some white low riding canvas pants with a multitude of pockets and the versatility to unzip the legs, converting them into shorts; she also bought some more conservative clothes just in case she chickened out. With a prank in mind, Nelly also bought three sets of thong panties. Then she couldn't resist checking out the computer department for a second just before rejoining the others. Nelly spent much of her spare time studying on the latest software and computer gadgets, something that most people found boring, before Abby came over to drag her back to the car.

As they returned to the parking lot, Nelly suddenly remembered that she had forgotten all about Steve. They had left him sleeping under her jacket in the front seat of the Cruiser in a lonely poorly lit abandoned parking lot. How safe was that? The other women, in a sleepy haze, not remembering much about the trip, failed to notice Steve; Abby panic when she first saw him and then remembered that he had joined them at the restaurant. While they were considering their circumstance an intimidating looking black and white police car, painted like it just drove out of a futuristic movie set, pulled up next to them.

"What are you ladies up to this time of night?" a blond headed police officer said through his window, bent on intimidating them.

"We're traveling to Florida, sir," Tracy said.

"Who's driving and who is that in the car?" By this time Steve had awoken, had come out from under Nelly's jacket and was opening the door.

Nelly stepped toward the window and said that she was the driver. In frustration, Nelly also said that Steve was her boyfriend…then she tried to explain… "not my boyfriend, boyfriend… but a friend that is a boy…I mean a man. Sir have we done something wrong?"

The police officer raises one of his eyebrows and came out of the black and white Dodge Challenger, then standing to his full uniformed height of over six foot he assessed the three women and the lone man. Determining that these ladies were probably someone's mothers, he felt safe enough. They couldn't be too bad being still dressed in work clothes. They reminded him somewhat of the music group *The Village People,* only a little more rag-tagged. Nelly wore a practical leisure pant suit, Tracy wore a dressy skirt and the other two wore steal toed boots and T-shirts with *Aviation World* written across the back.

He asked Nelly to take a sobriety test and Nelly was totally humiliated while being asked if she'd walk a straight line and then touched her nose with her eyes closed. She put her armload of bags down on the ground and complied with all his requests.

"I'm not drunk," she said scolding the officer, "just tired. Geeze, I can't get a break today."

"Listen Lady, just finish walking the line, or I'll arrest you for disorderly conduct."

"You can't do that, because I've done nothing wrong," she started to argue.

Steve could see where this was going and attempted at damage control by saying. "Please excuse my friend as she is a bit bitchy from a stressful day; however she is our designated driver and sober."

"OK, I see that she hasn't been drinking so I'm going to let her go. However, I suggest that you others get a room and clean up. You smell like a brewery and the next cop may not be so generous." Steve felt his ears burn. He wasn't even drinking and he didn't like being told he smelled. Abby was humiliated.

Tracy must have still been feeling the effects of alcohol because she was recklessly attracted to the hunky police officer. Catching his attention she batted her eyes and in her sexiest voice said, "God sure did make you good …sir…you are a *fine* look'n man."

Steve, Abby and Nelly's mouth's hung open at Tracy's friendly outburst toward the officer. This was totally out of character for Tracy's normally uptight personality.

To their disbelief the big cop turned red and grinned widely at Tracy as he ducked back into his car. As if on cue, the three of them turned their heads toward Tracy as if they didn't trust their ears. Tracy shrugged, threw her bags in the car and squeezed back into the backseat. "What?" She asked when they kept staring at her.

"A lot of firsts for you tonight, isn't there Tracy," Steve teased.

"He's right we need to clean up and rest, there's hotel down the block," Abby said as she pointed at a lighted sign that said *The Kumar Inn*.

"Let's stay there tonight and discuss this in the morning."

CHAPTER 9

The New Comer

As the four of them entered the hotel with their plastic bags in hand, they noticed that the hotel was surprisingly elegant for a small hotel. In the center of the lobby was a mosaic water fountain reaching up toward a domed ceiling with decorative paintings of exotic birds. A lounge in royal burgundy colors was off to one side and a granite covered check-in-desk to the other side. The smooth marble floors glistened with a fresh waxing reflecting the furnishings and the natural wooden pillars that held up the landing to the second floor.

The granite topped desk sat empty and abandoned, except for a few brochures and an old fashioned bell. Nelly rang the bell and immediately a dark headed young desk clerk who looked like she was the Indian princes in the story of *Aladdin's Lamp,* a Middle-Eastern Folktale passed down for generations, came bouncing out from somewhere behind the counter. She had a pencil tucked behind her right ear.

Against the three lady's protests, Steve gave the clerk his credit card. It was noticeable that he was impressed with the attractiveness of the young Indian woman behind the desk. She was very slender with long reflective black hair, a shiny complexion and dark sparkling eyes with thick lashes.

"Excuse me for not being at the desk, I'm studying for my hotel management exam," she apologized with a heavy Indian accent as she took the credit card and charged a room to it.

"Where are you people going?" she asked.

"I think that we are going to *Panama City Beach,* but it hasn't been fully discussed yet," Nelly looked thoughtfully toward the rest of them.

"You are?" the clerk asked excitedly, then "I need to go there in the morning and I've been looking for a ride."

This new turn of events was a little bit too strange for Nelly and she said, "Do you often hint to travel with strangers."

"No, you don't understand. 'I promised my Uncle Christopher Kumar, who manages *The Kumar Inn Beach Resort* that I would work for him the rest of the summer. 'I have been given a free double suite right on the beach facing the ocean that I really don't need because my Grandmother wants me to stay with her… *(she paused)*… oh boy, that will be interesting. 'Anyway, I can give the room to you as my guests if you people would like it for the weekend," she said desperately. "My cousin was supposed to drive me but he called to say that his automobile was in need of repair. 'The room includes a free continental breakfast and I'll throw in a Pizza too," she begged while thinking American's love pizza enough for her to sweeten the pot with the Italian bribe.

They all looked at each other and nodded. With a free room, it now seemed that it was fate and they were all meant to go to *Panama City Beach."*

"Well, what do you think?" Nelly asked the others.

"I think that it's a great idea!" again Tracy surprised everyone with her unusually agreeable nature.

Given that the desk clerk was beautiful, Steve was in total agreement. Abby just nodded her head.

Nelly looked at her watch, "Ok, just give our room a wakeup call in the morning around 7:00 a.m."

Abby counted on her fingers and said, "That's just five hours from now, is that enough sleep."

"That's all I ever sleep."

"My name is Lillian Kumar and I'll talk to you people in the morning," she said as she memorized their names on the registry. Then she gave Steve a furtive look, "I'll have someone bring you people coffee to your room in the morning but you'll have to come to the lobby for breakfast."

"Ok," Nelly agreed.

"My uncle will be forever grateful. My family will only let family members work the front desk."

When they reached the room, they were tired and the room seemed like an oasis in the desert. It was filled with cool air-conditioning and fresh smelling linen. There were two queen size beds calling them with a mound of soft, fluffy, pillows and white feathered comforters. There was a clean bathroom which none of them had seen since early Thursday morning; and in that bathroom was a stack of shampoo's, creams and soaps with a peach ribbons tied around soft looking washcloths. Steve didn't get a chance to relieve himself at Wal-Mart so he was first to use the bathroom. Abby and Tracy used their newly purchased toothbrushes and dressed in their new bed shirts: then they fell in the same bed together leaving Nelly a little flustered about having to crawl into the same bed as Steve.

Nelly had bought Steve some toiletries and summer shorts but she had forgotten to buy him something in which to sleep. Being the perfect gentleman, he stripped off his shirt and kept his pants on; his bare feet hung to the end of the bed.

Nelly cut her eyes sideways at Steve's six-pack and blew a deep breath out through her lips. His body was perfect!

"I saw that," Steve laughingly teased her.

"I'm not sure what to do with my hands," Nelly fesses up while turning bright red.

"Good save!" Tracy said sleepily, "I must confess that we all snuck a peak."

"Come on babies bring it on," Steve teased as he licked his fingers, pushed out his chest and touched his tits.

"I'm too tired to care," Nelly laughed as she threw a pillow over Steve's chest.

Steve rolled over and whispered to Nelly in the darkness, "I can't figure you out, you're like an enigma, you know how to flirt, but it also embarrasses you. 'Don't be embarrassed, I enjoy it."

Nelly didn't know what to make of Steve, why did he feel he had to tell her that? Were they becoming friends and he felt the need to say it's OK to be herself. Oh God help me, she thought, as she realized that he was so sexy laying their next to her. If he only knew what she was really thinking, he'd be the one turning red. She reminded herself over and over in her mind…married, married…he's too young…he's too young…

Abby broke through the tension when she said, "OK, settle down you two and nobody criticize me for snoring."

Tracy laughed and said, "I hope I don't fart in my sleep."

Steve grinned and said, "I didn't think that you little ladies talked so vulgar but now that you've broke the ice."

The women all yelled, "NO!"

"Isn't it nice to be ourselves for a change, People have forgotten how to have fun these days," Tracy said through a yawn.

"Shut up and go to sleep, Tracy," Abby demanded.

CHAPTER 10

The Chase Begins

David McMillan stepped off the plane in Atlanta at 7 a.m. the next morning and took the people moving Tran to baggage claim. From there, he took the bus to the Rent-A-Car place and rented a green Honda Accord. Because the airport was close to Nelly's work, he decided to drive there first to see what Adam Wooddale had to say about Nelly's impulsive decision to take her workmates to Florida. He wanted to put Adam on the spot in order to explain his actions.

Adam didn't invite David to talk in his office as he felt it was not appropriate to discuss Nelly's suspension with someone outside the company. At this time Adam was feeling a bit silly about the whole thing but it was too late to recall everyone back to work. It was all a misunderstanding and sometimes tempers get in the way of good judgment. Even Heather seemed to calm down.

"Mr. Wooddale, did you know that your employees, along with my wife, decided to drive to Florida yesterday as a result of your obvious poor judgment?" David said, more of an accusation then question.

"Mr. McMillan, no disrespect, but it's not company policy to discuss our employees with outsiders—even if they are family members," Adam wisely retorted. "We stand by our decisions and where employees go on their own time is none of our business."

Then Adam attempted to console David briefly, "I'm sure they will be fine," David was taller than Adam but Adam was not intimidated.

"Well, I will let you know NOW that if anything happens to my wife, I will sue this company for the emotional distress you've caused me—do you understand that," David's face turned red with anger as he pointed a finger in Adams face.

"Mr. McMillan, I will have to ask you to leave now before I call the police," Adam looked at him with no fear in his eyes.

"I can't believe that she defended you, you're nothing but an asshole!" he yelled at Adam.

As David stormed out of the lobby, Adam wondered what Mr. McMillan meant by Nelly defending him. Somehow that consoled his troubled mind in knowing that she would defend him in these circumstances. He hadn't slept all night while trying to second guess himself and also in evaluating whether he had handled a bad situation with the skill required of a good supervisor. What other actions should he have taken? In his world of being a boss there was many hard decisions for which life never prepared him. He felt that he had to always keep both the employee's welfare and *Aviation World*'s welfare in mind at the same time: sometimes it seemed a contradiction and impossible to juggle. What was good for the company wasn't always easy for the employees; the dilemma was that without the company, there would be no jobs and without the employees there would be no product.

Adam took a deep breath as he watched the green Honda speed out of the parking lot. Poor Nelly, he thought, she has her hands full with him.

****

A CHANGE OF LUCK

David picked up his cell phone and called Neal to tell him that he was on the way home to their Atlanta residence. Neal was already hard at work trying to trouble shoot in finding a motor mount for another Nissan Aero and wasn't in the mood for his father's ranting.

"Relax Dad, Mom will come home when she is ready. 'She works hard and takes care of everyone—maybe she needs to run away for little while to get her head on straight, " he said distracted by the parts catalog sitting on the counter in front of him. He had to get the part numbers right or they would send the wrong part so it was an irritating distraction to be drug into his parents problems. He had problems of his own.

"I don't know how she could do this to me," he seemed to be more worried about himself.

Neal suddenly became angry which took his attention away from the catalog, "she isn't doing anything to you and would you stop making everything about you. Mom has been tired and out of it lately—like there is a lot on her mind. 'Let her go have some fun. 'She'll probably be a better for it. 'Dad I really can't get into the middle of this."

"I think she is having an affair," David blurted out ignoring Neal's anger.

"How do you know? 'She doesn't have time to have an affair …she's probably going to go down to Florida and will end up at Wal-Mart or Best Buy in the computer department. 'Mom is nothing more than a boring, middle-aged, computer geek who pays more attention to the latest web editing tools than anything else—she wouldn't know what to do with a man…now get a hold of yourself, Dad. 'Now I really have to go," Neal said as he hung up frustrated with his father.

His supervisor, Roger, heard the phone conversation and looked at Neal with questions in his eyes. Neal just shrugged and uttered, "Parents, can't live with them and can't live without them." They laughed at his joke.

After David hung up with Neal, he wondered if Neal would ever do better than a mechanics job. It was embarrassing but Nelly insisted that they should be proud of Neal's hard work. Although, in contradiction, he was very proud of Neal for all that he had accomplished. At birth they didn't even think that he would live, let alone thrive.

David decided that it was time to go after Nelly. He fully intended on dragging her back home where she belonged—and it was time for her to quit her job.

After David arrived at the big brick home where they lived most of their married life, he immediately went to Nelly's book lined study and signed on to her computer to check their bank accounts. The computer sat on a newly dusted desk smelling of lemon polish. The desk was under the only window in the room to keep it well lit for Nelly's hobby of computer programming. As he waited for the computer to open the website to the bank account he observed the line of nineteen matching books sitting on her shelves, Nelly's collection from her favorite author, they were all in alphabetical order and lovingly kept dust free. Well at least she has good taste in authors, David thought.

Nelly wasn't much of a housekeeper but they were lucky enough to afford Jennifer, a young mother of three who needed a job to work around her children's schedule, so she did house cleaning.

After opening Nelly's bank account, he noticed nothing there to indicate her making any charges so he opened their joint account. He saw a charge in *Montgomery, Alabama* for gas at a Wal-Mart at 1:05 a.m.

He queried for a few hotels in the nearby vicinity just in case, on a whim, she decided to stay the night. The last hotel on he called was *The Kumar Inn* which was only a block away from the Wal-Mart. It was nine a.m. in the morning, eight a.m. Alabama time, when he called to ask desk clerk if she had stayed there. The desk clerk said that he did know her because she was giving his cousin Lillian a ride to *Panama City Beach."*

"Who was with her," he asked.

"Umm, I don't really know their names. I can look them up...let's see. 'There is a Nelly McMillan, Tracy Malone..., Abby Winters....and a Steve Jones...," the clerk told him helpfully.

Without saying thank you he hung up the phone wondering who Steve Jones was...he suspected that it was an alias. This is just getting worse, he thought as he went to their bedroom and dug through the bedside table looking for the Browning Automatic Pistol made in the year 1909 that Nelly's father gave her when she was just a girl. The pistol was only as big as his palm, and worth something to gun collectors as an antique, but it still worked perfectly at the gun range—so Nelly kept it by her bed for protection. It shot .32 caliber bullets which she kept in another drawer with the strange reasoning that if the gun should become stolen, the bullets would be harder to find.

He packed a few things from a black marble topped dresser and then headed south on the expressway to Alabama.

CHAPTER 11

On to the Beach

 Friday Morning, being an hour behind in Alabama, the clock showed eight a.m. when Lillian was ready. Lillian had sent the promised wake-up call at seven a.m. but she had a couple of things to finish and then needed to pack so she informed the small group that it would be another hour. That would give the four them time to bathe and eat before they all started down highway 431 south. It was a pretty straight shot to *Panama City Beach* but Nelly decided to walk to a nearby gas station to buy a map anyway, so she could do some trip planning. She knew that she should break down and buy a G.P.S but somehow honing her skills in the interpretation of maps seemed much more challenging. Being computer savvy, she usually preferred electronic automation but this was different. She also wanted to buy a six pack of cold cokes, a cooler to keep them in and a few snacks.

 Meanwhile, not nearly as ambitious, Tracy and Abby were sitting in the lounge area enjoying their continental breakfast when the police officer from the night before entered. Tracy gasped and hid behind Abby hoping to get out of direct eyesight but it was too late as he had already noticed the two of them. He pored himself a cup of hazelnut coffee with no cream and sugar and walked toward them.

As he passed the attendant preparing the breakfast, she greeted him with a jolly, "Good morning Ed, how are you today?"

"Good, and you?" he returned with a wide bright smile which took Tracy's breath away.

The attendant looked toward the two women and explained Ed's appearance, "Mr. Stewart comes in for a cup of hazelnut coffee every morning after his shift. He keeps an eye on the hotel at night so we repay his kindness with his favorite, a waffle with blueberry syrup and hazelnut coffee. We make the waffles up fresh for the guests. Would you like one?"

Abby declined for the both of them. The hardboiled eggs and cream cheese beagles had filled them up.

Tracy said under her voice, "Why doesn't he be a good boy and go to a doughnut shop like every other self respecting police officer."

"I heard that and a jolly good morning to you lady's…are you feeling any better?" he asked Abby with a big grin on his face.

Tracy suddenly embarrassed that he overheard her distracted herself by fiddling with her beagle. She felt hot sitting near the window with the sun beaming in… or was it something else.

Abby just nodded her head.

"Here, here and I thought that God had made me real good… and that I was REAL fine look'n," he mimicked Tracy while enjoying making Tracy squirm.

Abby snickered while moving back out of the way of the line sight, "That sure did come back to bite you."

Tracy put her elbows on the table and hid her face in a pair of cupped hands. After a moment, she looked up into his handsome features haloed by his thick blond hair to apologized, "I'm sorry for my rudeness, I've a slight headache and I'm a bit out of sorts this morning."

He turned the chair around and straddled it as he sat across from her. "I believe that I'm used to ladies insulting me by now. I've been in the business of listening to insults for about eighteen years."

"No," Abby looked surprised, "you don't look old enough to have been in it ten years."

"Oh really now, well it must be my "fine look'n" baby face," he laughed.

"I said that I was sorry," Tracy said defensively.

"It's OK lady, I hope that you don't mind me joining you this morning. I thought you all were pretty cute last night. You looked like a drunken rag-tag version of an old rock band. You look better this morning…I hope that you feel better."

He assessed Tracy, still stylish looking in her baby blue Wal-Mart sun dress with tiny pink flowers. She truly was a very stunning women and gracefully tall. He turned his chair around to sit straight and thought that it was sad that these ladies were probably just passing through. They seemed fun and he would like the opportunity to get to know them better. He remembered that Tracy's driver's license indicated that she was nine year older than him but age wasn't an issue with him. If a woman was beautiful both inside and out, who cared?

Abby and Ed started talking amongst themselves. It was really getting on Tracy's nerves so she tried to act interested in her breakfast.

"Well, I'm going back to my room and freshen up," Tracy finally couldn't stand it any longer. As she started to rise from her seat, Ed put a large gentle hand on her shoulder and stopped her from standing.

For a minute Tracy didn't understand the gesture but then she saw Lillian waving from the front door toward them. Ed said, "I think that Lillian is trying to get your attention."

Oh someone has got my attention alright Tracy thought as she assessed the sheer size of Ed's hands: She tried not to wonder if he was that big all over.

Lillian left her suitcase by the door and on slender gazelle like legs ran over to their table while saying, "I'm ready when you people are ready."

"I don't know where Steve and Nelly went but they should show up soon," Abby offered.

Just then Nelly walked through the door juggling a small cooler and a sack; all the while trying to fold a fairly large and uncooperative paper map—Steve had been on his morning jog and coincidently ran in behind her with nothing but a pair of shorts on. He had a perspiration running down a smooth muscular chest. Every woman in the lobby took notice—but Nelly who was still fumbling with the map.

"There they are now; I'll show you to the car so you can put your suitcase away," Tracy said, glad to have an excuse to get away.

It took a half an hour to organize everyone and get them into the car. Steve insisted on driving but Nelly liked to drive so she refused. Tracy, Lillian and Abby sat in the back seat while Steve still again sat up front.

CHAPTER 12

Fantasies

As they drove down the road, Nelly had a sudden thought. "What if everyone picked a fantasy, something you'd never dream in your wildest imagination that you'd accomplish, and made that fantasy came true this week?" She decided to find out what each person wished for and do her best to try and make it come true.

"If only that could come true but all my fantasies involve lots of green stuff and none of us are rich enough to just through money away," Tracy said realistically.

"That's true, but we can all still pick something that's not all that expensive and still obtainable but fun," Nelly defended her idea.

"Well my fantasy is NOT to jump out of a plane or anything that involves personal danger or water," Abby laughed.

"Oh come on now, Nelly has a point," Steve defended Nelly's Idea, "If you think hard enough there has to be something fun to do this week and set a goal to do it. It doesn't mean that it would be your only fantasy, just one of them. OK I'll start—Like it's not realistic to expect to remarry again to a readymade family because I'm too old to start over; but I wouldn't mind taking a sea plane tour along the beach to see what it looks like from above. 'I've fixed a lot small aircraft parts but I've never been in one."

"Ah that's sweet, and I've always wanted a fuck'n threesome," Abby teased.

"Abby, be real, and don't forget about Lillian, she doesn't need to hear your foul mouth," Tracy scolded. Sometimes, Abby could be disgusting when she gets to cussing, Tracy thought.

"I'm used to it, I have a grandmother that can put Abby to shame," Lillian said under her breath.

They thought Lillian's assessment of her grandmother to be a little curious but didn't question her.

"Aren't we a bunch of screwed up old women...and gentlemen," Nelly laughed, "It's usually the men that want a threesome and the women who want to fly somewhere."

The miles creped by as they sat quietly pondering fantasies and wondering at the possibilities. The roadside scenery was turning from pine forests to swamps and then to barbed plants and prickly brush growing in the sand.

Lillian broke the silence and proclaimed that she wanted to choose her own husband. "Indians have a network of other Indians and they all decide who the women in the family should marry. I want to be like you people and decide on my own husband."

"Yes," said Nelly, "and you should be able to decide.

"Ok, while we are dreaming, I would like to remarry my Ex," Tracy blurted out and everyone reacted with a loss for words.

Nelly broke the silence, "Ok, Tracy that was an uncomfortable moment, but at least your facing it now."

"What is your fantasy Nelly," Steve changed the subject.

"I don't know…I think that this is it ….that is to shake things up and have an adventure with my friends."

"No you can't get off that easy," Abby wouldn't let Nelly off the hook.

"Well I know that this sounds so Cliché or passé but I would like to dance in the moonlight on the beach with a handsome gentleman," Nelly said dreamily.

"What?" Abby acted shocked, "You be real…no it's not…your fantasy is to write the ultimate computer program or write a book about computer shortcuts?"

"Well that too…but I was trying to pick a somewhat obtainable goal," she said as she realized that Abby could see right through her attempt to appease everyone. The fantasy about dancing in the moonlight was real enough but it was Nelly's dream to invent a program on the computer that would take off in the market. She spent hours clicking away and writing the language for an avionics parts inventory program for large businesses. Nelly had a quite a few ideas toward programmed games and data bases but nothing ever became of them. It wasn't the money but the challenge that she wanted most….however, money would be good too.

Nelly's cell phone rang and she could see it was her husband on the caller I.D. She decided to ignore it until she had time to talk in private. She didn't feel like arguing with him right now in front of her friends. She hit the ignore button.

"I'm sorry but I'm sticking to the threesome fantasy," Abby said and they all laughed.

Well that's the end of that idea, Nelly thought. It was a dumb idea anyway. No way could they re-unite Tracy with her Ex-husband and she certainly wasn't going to encourage a threesome with Abby. However, knowing Abby like she did, she knew that Abby was just joking. Her worldly act was usually just a façade.

As they came closer to *Panama City Beach*, they started to see big signs advertizing a tour company called *Fun-n-wet* who offered sea plane and air boat adventures. Nelly looked at Steve with a "will wonders never cease" look—as they were just talking about the subject—and asked, "Well why not?"

"I don't know," he said, "I don't think that the other ladies would be interested."

"The sign also says that there is a restaurant near the tour place with fish and lobster, let's go eat mass quantities of sea food until we bust and then decide," Nelly suggested.

"Anyway, we all need a bathroom break and something real to drink. All Nelly brought were sodas and water, I need a beer." Abby seemed to be the first to get tired of the coziness of the car.

It was nearly lunch time and everyone was hungry so they took the road leading to *The Boon Docks*. At first the long the driveway seemed like a seedy area of town with run down trailers attached to rusty natural gas tanks: but, as they drove further, the charm of the area started to grow on them. It was like time stood still and everything still looked as it did twenty or thirty years ago, only rustier. Soon they pulled up to a bay with several wooden buildings surrounding a small dock. As they rolled up into the gravel parking lot Nelly noticed the sign to the restaurant over the top of a large grey shack with decks and fishing nets surrounding it. Star fish, large corks with hooks and fishing paraphernalia hung from the nets. She could here live music and seagulls. Just as the five of them started following the music, an older gentleman waved them down from the direction of the green shack nearest the dock; he looked to be in his seventies but of good health as his steps quickly took him to the parking for the purpose of greeting the four of them. He was wearing a yellow T-shirt which had the picture of a seaplane on it and the words *Fun-n-wet* arched over the top of the seaplane.

"Hi, my name is Richard, where are you folks from?" he asked while he held an arthritic riddled hand out to Steve to be shook.

Steve didn't expect the sudden friendliness of Richard and shook his hand without question.

Nelly also reached out to shake Richard's hand gently in fear of hurting him and answered his question, "We're form Atlanta on a little vacation."

"The restaurant is a good place to go eat," Richard recommended, "Me and my wife eat there a lot in-between tours. I built the dock over there and started me a small tour business. I used to be a pilot for the commercial airline industry way back when but I like the freedom of living here, so I started this business. It's a beautiful place," he signed with a faraway look as the breeze lifted a strain of white hair over sparking green eyes.

"How did you build that dock under water?" Steve asked as the four of them all walked toward it.

"I used to have a trailer up there on the hill," he said pointing up at a wooded area, "and then one season the bay was low enough to sink pylons in some cement. I built the decking on it," he said proudly. I figured that the water level would rise again and it did. You see all this used to be basically a marsh area before we developed it." Being there was mostly trailers; Steve saw the visual of the land being developed from a trailer park to a small purposely looking run down business. It being developed was questionable as it was now looking just a step above the previously mentioned trailer park; the boon dock theme was perfect.

As they rounded the small reception shack they all recognized a white Cessna 180k on Aeorcet 3500 floats rocking up and down in the bay waters at the end of the dock. They had seen many pictures of it but never up close and personal. Nelly and Steve looked at each other in excitement.

"Richard… how much is it for the tour for the five of us?" Steve thought that he would wheel and deal a little.

"Oh no you don't," Abby said. "I'm not afraid of water but I don't like water; you can't even get me over water."

Tracy ignored Abby and offered some information about them to Richard, "We all work in aviation…Abby and Steve here could have possibly worked on some of the units in your cockpit."

"Really, what's the name of your company?"

"It's…ah… *Aviation World,"* she said as she wondered if should say "is" or "was."

"I've heard of it, they did an inspection on a gyro for me," Richard said making conversation.

"Lillian here doesn't work with us, she is only along for the ride," Steve changed the subject. He wasn't in the mood to talk shop.

Richard eyed the five of them, assessing their combined weight and their ability to step up into a plane. It was his job to pick out the weakest link in case of an emergency in the air. Two of the women were stylishly dressed in sun dresses, Nelly wore a pair of white shorts and Abby sported army fatigues. He guessed correctly that Nelly was the oldest but she seemed quite fit for her age and looked quit fetching to his aged eyes. He guessed that it was probably from years of exercise or from jogging. Of course, Richard thought, in his seventy plus years, anyone younger than him looked quite fetching. His beautiful wife was just sixty-five and she was the most beautiful women in the world to him. She handled the other end of the tour business: that was the Jet Ski tours and air boat rides.

"Well, look, I don't want to keep you folks from your lunch. After you eat, you all consider a tour if you feel up to it. I have sea plane rides and my wife will take you either in an air boat or on a Jet Ski tour across the bay into the swampy marsh to see the Osprey and alligators, you hear. I'll give you a good price." Richard had a broad smile on his face as he shook their hands again and walked back to the little green building where a sun backed, older women was leaning over a cooler.

"I think that this nice gentleman spoke to us more because he is just friendly rather than really needing the business. 'He is probably old enough to sell his business and retire," Lillian guessed.

"Well I for one am not interested in seeing alligators, in case you didn't know it, they eat people," Tracy said with a shutter.

They continued following the music which took them to a deck facing the bay. The music was coming from a blond lady sitting against the building strumming an *Ovation* guitar hooked up to a P.A. and two free standing speakers. She was singing her version of *Down in Margaretaville, by Jimmy Buffet* which was quit unique and very good. The five of them sat down at a table which looked like it came from the timbers of an old sunken ship. A friendly attendant, dressed like a deck hand, ducked under the fishing nets and asked if they wanted some drinks while they were looking at the menu. The friends all agreed that a pitcher of frozen Margaritas would be nice, except Abby wanted a cold beer, Lillian wanted hot tea and Nelly wanted her Margarita a virgin. That left Steve and Tracy to share the pitcher.

As they sat sipping their drinks Nelly said, "This IS a fantasy. We are overlooking the ocean bay, smelling the fresh salty air and we still have a whole two weeks off in which to look forward."

"A toast," Steve called out as he raised his glass, "To good friends and to getting drunk."

They all laughed and raised their glasses. Lillian raised her china tea cup which looked ridiculous.

They ordered a huge sampler tray and shared it. Lillian and Nelly chow down on the coleslaw while the others sampled shrimp, lobster, crab-cakes, Alaska snow crab legs and fried fish of the day from the bay. It came with deliciously greasy fries, onion rings and crispy hush puppies.

"Well what about it Steve, I'll go with you on that sea plane ride if you like?" Nelly volunteered.

"First we'll go alligator trolling in the swamp across the bay and then we'll fly and see the beach from the air. 'The other ladies can drive on into *Panama City Beach* and settle into the hotel; then come back and pick us up in several hours....please," she begged.

He looked skeptical.

"It will be my treat," Nelly sweetened the pot.

He considered the expense that they were about to make. He wasn't sure he felt comfortable with her paying his way but he was a divorced man with child support. They had come this far so why not just a little further. Besides, Nelly could afford it, her husband made a bunch of money.

"Alright, you're on," he said as he gulped the remainder of his margarita down.

Nelly picked up the tab for everyone by using her shared debit card account. She convinced herself that David wouldn't mind. She'd call him tonight and explain everything.

After paying the bill they sat there for a few more minutes taking in the view, the music and the fresh smell of the salt water. The blond singer obviously took a shine to Steve and brought her perfectly sun kissed body to the table to talk to the audience of four women and one man. Nelly admired her sailor style red stripped shirt and the red, white and blue sequences on the back pocket of her blue jeans.

"Hi my name is Julia are you all enjoying yourselves?" she greeted them with a sweet southern accent.

"Nice to meet you Julia…that's also my daughter's name," Nelly said with honesty.

"Nice to meet you…you're pretty good," Steve complimented her in his low manly voice.

"Steve here plays and sings too," Nelly volunteered and the rest just nodded.

"Hey, why don't you all come up here and sing a song for the audience," the blond singer coxed Steve to get up and sing.

After a few minutes of hesitation and argument they were able to convince Steve to give it a try.

He knew a lot of songs but all he could think of on the spot was, *House of the Rising Sun,* which was originally an old folk song written by an unknown. This went over real well with the ladies as his attractive low voice and skill with the guitar impressed even the blond singer. The next song he played was a guitar solo in a classical style and everyone clapped as his fingers skillfully ran over the strings. Then he humbly nodded his head to thank the audience before putting the guitar down. He wanted to hear the ladies critique him, in hopes that it was favorably and he didn't make a fool out of himself.

"I enjoyed that," he told them all as Julia went back to work singing. "Speaking of fantasies, I always wanted to perform in front of a crowd that would listen to my rambling."

"You're quite good and we enjoyed it very much, I'm glad that you and Hanna exchanged phone numbers," Lillian said a little star struck with his ability.

After the women all bragged on Steve, they decided that it was time to take Lillian to her grandmothers so she could rest up for the night shift. She hadn't slept since yesterday and she was looking a little bedraggled.

After they said their goodbyes to Tracy, Abby and Lillian, Nelly drug Steve back over to the Green shack on the homemade dock to buy tickets for both the Jet Ski tour and the sea plane ride.

CHAPTER 13

David Arrives

David pulled the 2010 Honda up to the police station in *Montgomery, Alabama*. He had gone to the hotel and found out that Nelly had left over four hours ago. David was one of those types of visitors that could make it a bad day for the desk clerk of *The Kumar Inn*. David demanded to have Nelly's room number: then accused the poor guy of withholding information. When the clerk threatened to have him removed by the police, David calmed down and left peacefully, but the desk clerk had given him an idea.

He punched in a request for the nearest police station in the G.P.S. and followed the directions. He parked his car on the street in front and then went inside to calmly stride up to the thick glass plated reception window and talk to a young uniformed lady sporting head phones.

Looking genuinely concerned he told the receptionist manning the window that he thought that his wife maybe kidnapped by a Steve Jones. She pointed to a chair in the waiting room saying, "Sir would you please wait in the chair over there and I'll have officer Dunwoody come out and take a statement." When a husband comes to make a claim such as this, it was often did not end well. When a woman disappears she usually turned up dead.

Officer Dunwoody was a big guy with a thick gray wreath of hair wrapped around a bald head and a big belly hanging over his belt. He was comfortably jacketless with a white shirt, loose red tie and an occupied shoulder harness. His tie clip was that of a gold plated shield saying thirty-five years and looked like a gift indicating that he was nearing retirement.

"My name is Detective Jack Dunwoody, I understand your wife is missing," he said as he reached out to shake David's hand but David ignored it.

"Yes, she has been missing since yesterday around noon," he acted the desperate man. "I'm from Memphis and she is from Atlanta. 'I traced her here through bank charges to a hotel named *The Kumar Inn* but lost her trail."

"I didn't catch your name?" Jack wanted to get first things first.

"David McMillan."

"Ok Mr. McMillan, let's start from the beginning and see if we can work this out," said Detective Jack Dunwoody as he observed David signs of a lie. Many police officers went to classes in none verbal communication; communications such as if a suspect was telling the truth they usually looked away toward the right, or left, he couldn't remember. David was looking left. However, not in every case was this perfect science.

"Along with two other employees, she was put on suspension yesterday at her job in Atlanta. 'I found online in my bank account a charge at *McMulligan's Bar and Grill* near the airport and then the next charge was at a Wal-Mart here in *Montgomery* at 1:00 a.m. or so—this morning. '*The Kumar Inn* said that some guy named Steve Jones had checked in with her and her friends. 'Nelly would never drive this far without telling me something. I'm her husband and she tells me everything. 'I tell you she must be kidnapped," David told the story while looking did his best in the role of a poor distraught husband.

"Ok, do you know if Nelly is in her own vehicle or did her vehicle turn up somewhere?"

"I don't know but her tag is GA 555," he said sounding helpless. With half the police force out to find her, this will teach her lesson to not to run off without telling him, he thought.

"If you'll excuse me a minute, I'll go back to my desk and put this in the computer to see if her car has turned up anywhere," Detective Dunwoody said politely.

Back at his desk, Jack punched in Nelly's P.T. Cruiser's tag number and it collaborated David's story of Nelly being in *Montgomery*. Officer, Ed Stewart, Jack's friend and coworker, had pulled the Cruiser over around 1:30 a.m. and ran a tag of a P.T Cruiser matching Mr. McMillan's description. The report said that it seemed to be a small party but there weren't any drugs or open cans of alcohol. The driver was Nelly McMillan whose story panned out as being the designated driver. Although her friend's were considered suspicious of alcohol abuse, the drive was sober so Ed let them go.

Jack Dunwoody thought, that he'd better call Ed and find out if Ed knew anything concerning Mr. McMillan's claim.

Post leaving the hotel, Ed had gone home. After showering, he laid down while fully dressed in a freshly washed white T-Shirt and a pair of denim blue jeans. When Ed worked the night shift, he rarely used either bed in his two bedroom condominium. Day time sleep always seemed more like a long nap rather than a good night's sleep and when he napped, he slept on the sofa. He never had to set the alarm because he only slept five hours at a time: then he'd wake on his own. He'd only been asleep for three hours when the sound of the phone ringing sent him into a panic and he rolled off the sofa while reaching for the phone. Sleeping three hours was only enough sleep to make a man angry.

"Hello," Ed said groggily to his old mentor and friend.

"Hey Ed, sorry to wake you," Officer Dunwoody said genuinely sorry as he knew what it was like.

"This better be good, Jack," Ed halfway teased.

"I have a question about the P.T. Cruiser you stopped in the Wal-Mart parking lot last night with the license plate GA 555. 'I have a Mr. David McMillan here at the station filing a missing report for a Nelly McMillan. 'Can you enlighten me on her behavior last night?"

Ed asked Jack to hold on a second while he got up off the floor to position himself back up on the sofa. He took a sip out of a bottle of Deer Park water and, having gotten his wits about him, picked up the phone again.

"What does Mr. McMillan say?" Jack's experienced mentoring had taught Ed not to give up too much information until he knew details and, in this case, Ed applied Jack's own advice against him.

"Nothing other than that she went missing yesterday around noon after being suspended from her job; he said that she was with two girlfriends and a Steve Jones. 'He said that he followed her check card charges here," Jack repeated what David had told him.

"I also saw them this morning at *The Kumar Inn* and they seemed fine to me," Ed said confused at why this man would file his wife as missing. "As a matter of fact, Nelly McMillan was driving the car. 'I think that this may be a simple case of a jealous husband."

"I think that you're probably right but let's go ahead and investigate," Being Ed's superior it was Jack's call.

"Well… can you convince him to check into a local hotel for twenty-four hours on some story of being here to identify his wife once she is found; in the meantime, can you get a search warrant for his car," Ed wanted to take this seriously before it got out of hand.

"I did think about it and I agree; your afraid that he may be gunning for her and using us to find her," Jack was always a quick study.

"It's probably nothing but we better cross our t's and dot our i's. 'Ninety percent of the time it turns out to be a guilty husband when a woman has gone missing," Ed said as he thought about the other two women who he feared might get in the middle of a domestic dispute, Tracy in particular.

Then Ed said, "What are you going to tell him?"

Jack answered, "I'm going to tell him the truth—which it is routine to rule out the husband on missing cases."

Ed hung up the phone while trying to sort this all out in his mind. He wondered if he missed something last night and this morning. Was Nelly being held against her will? If she had been abducted, it just didn't make sense for her to have been driving the vehicle last night and then this morning wondering around the hotel by herself. Beyond his normal duty, he stayed out of domestic cases but something about this one seemed personal; maybe it's' because he actually talked to the victim or victims. He thought about Tracy.

CHAPTER 14

Fun-n-wet

The five of them parted ways in *The Boone Docks* parking lot where Nelly gave Abby the keys to the little Cruiser and then, along with Steve, they walked over to the dock holding the Cessna 180k and several upgraded Jet Ski's. Who they supposed was Richard's wife stopped cleaning some windows facing the bay and welcomed them with a big broad smile. She had fine auburn hair tucked in a bun and her long slender short clad legs were blackened by constant exposure to the sun. One would be shock to learn that she was in her mid sixties as the outdoor lifestyle of a tour guide suited her well. All the warnings against sun exposure didn't apply to her as her skin was smooth and wrinkle free. The dock that was built straight up to the front of the paint chipped door, it vibrated slightly under her feet as she walked over and shook their hands.

"I'm Rebecca and my husband over there is Richard, he had forty years experience flying if you're interested in a seaplane ride?" she started her sales pitch as she pointed at Richard who was at the end of the dock examining his plane, "The plane is a new toy for him, the old one was a good one but we parked it."

"Well, actually it says that we can have a Jet Ski tour too, what is that all about?" Nelly asked.

Rebecca looked pleased, "For seventy dollars each I can take you across the bay to see the dolphins and then into the swamps over there to see the wild life." She pointed to the other side of the bay, "A lot of people come to see the alligators and the Osprey nests."

Steve looked uncomfortable as he wasn't sure that he wanted to go trolling amongst the alligators but Nelly seemed excited so he tried to act bravely. He didn't want to be out shown by a slip of women five years older than himself.

"How about the seaplane ride, is it safe?" Nelly asked.

"Sure honey," Rebecca said with encouragement, "Like I said, Richard has forty years experience and the whole bay—and the whole ocean beyond—is one big landing field. You couldn't be safer."

Steve and Nelly thought a minute.

"I'll tell you what, we would normally charge one-hundred-fifty each for both tours but for each of you I'll only charge one-hundred-twenty-five," Rebecca said in hopes of helping them to make up their minds. However, their minds were already made up. Nelly and Steve wanted an adventurous afternoon.

"We'll take it," Nelly said and followed Rebecca inside to pay in advance by check card. Meanwhile Steve walked down to the Cessna to admire the plane. It was new and being an avionics man he wanted to see the cockpit and talk shop for a minute.

Calling Steve back, Nelly explained that there was a locker for their paraphernalia like watches and cell phones; also that they had to sign a waiver toward injuries.

"It's a good idea not to take cell phones in the swamp and get them wet," Rebecca explained and then assured them, "I do have flares in case we become stranded but we won't go far enough into the swamp to worry about it and I've never been stranded." .

Soon Nelly and Steve were on the Jet Ski's taking lessons on how the small machines works. They each had a safety bracelets attached to an off switch so the ski would turn itself off if they fell in the water. They also they learned to juice up the gas to make sudden turns and that it would right itself if the Jet Ski tipped over. Finally, life jacket clad, with a bottles of water as their only survival kit, they sped off across the bay with a Fun misty spray coming off the front of the Jet Ski bathing them. The three of them happily skied freely across waves of the bay with Rebecca as their guide. Nelly was the only one uptight about falling in the water and sat stiffly on her seat.

In the middle of the bay Rebecca held up her hand in a signal to stop and the Jet Ski's all stopped around each other. As they sat silently, she pointed to a ripple in the water where a dolphin's nose peak through the surface of the water. Then she explained in her professional tour guide voice, "Under us is a group of dolphins that live in the bay. If you look close you'll see several babies alongside their mothers. They probably won't show off too much for you in order to protect the babies but they are curious and will hang around you for a moment."

Steve and Nelly sat quietly rocking in the waves farther away from shore than either of them had ever been; meanwhile, studying the waters around them for dolphins. As they studied the murky water several large shadowy shapes appeared to pass by just inches just under the surface. Dolphins were probably an everyday occurrence to Rebecca but it was a wondrous site to Steve and Nelly and they felt like the explorer Crusoe studying the habits of the some mysterious mammals under the sea. Nelly wanted this moment to last forever and wondered if she jumped into the bay waters would the dolphins play with her? Sitting on a Jet Ski miles from the shore made her feel like microscopic ameba in a blue-grey universe of water, and she thought how wondrous was God's plan. Then she thought that she would have to use her graphics program to create a dolphin screen saver on her computer at home. He would be eternally swimming through the miles of water.

"Damn that's cool," Steve was overwhelmed. Nelly wondered which part was the coolest for him, the Jet Ski or the dolphins.

"Let's move on as we have another thirty minutes to go before we are finished crossing the bay, we have to mind the ecologist and stay within the designated pylons so follow me; and Nelly relax, the whole ocean bay is a safety net," Rebecca said as she again started her Jet Ski. Looking back at the two of them she noticed the smiles of happy customers and decided that she like the two of them. She wondered how they were related or knew each other. Richard usually had the scoop on all his customers but he hadn't had time to talk to Rebecca about it.

Nelly felt like she was in an action movie and could imagine flying across the bay on Jet Ski's while running away from villains, bullets riddling the water next to her. Nelly had a vivid imagination that never ceased, even as she grew into her middle age. She had a graphic arts program on her computer at home that would allow her to create a video game to mirror this trip; her home made video games weren't good enough for public use but her five year old grandson, Christian loved them.

As Rebecca signaled to stop on the other side of the bay in front of the entrance of the swamp Nelly looked at Steve and said, "Stirred not shaken or is it shaken not stirred when referencing martinis?" Steve caught onto her corny reference right away and humored her by saying, "Well, I wouldn't care right now as long as it had lots of ice, it's hot as you-know-what out here." They laughed at their foolishness but Rebecca continued the tour speech.

The early afternoon sun was getting hotter by the minute and Steve was beginning to wish he had worn a baseball cap. He didn't know if it was the heat or the ocean humidity that made him sweaty.

"First we'll take a drink of water to stay hydrated. 'Then watch for my hands as we go into the swamp while I use the signals I taught in our lessons to indicate you need to speed up or slow down. 'There are speed limits and noise limits applied to several sections where people and animals live. 'When we move further down river I'll try to slow you down to point out the wild life and alligators; please pay close attention as these areas are policed and local authorities will stop our tours if we are too noisy," she warned. "Alligators will generally leave you alone but some facts on them are that they can stay under water for hours and they can jump up out of the water to expose something like seventy or eighty percent of their body mass. 'Watch carefully along the banks as they can blend into the foliage."

At first the tour didn't seem too remote as they slowly passed under an old train trestle and then passed a line of old southern mansions. Neatly cut lawns stopped at the edge of the river bank which was held back by either tar covered rail road ties or cement walls to keep the banks from slipping into the marshy river. Several homes had small docks for fishing and boating. After passing the houses it became nothing more than a marsh thick with roots and grasses growing straight up out of large pools of water. Some sections of the river were heavy in isolated trees while other sections were just marshy and grassy. Rebecca signaled to speed up until they came to a dip in the river's edge. There Rebecca pointed to a lone tree trunk petrified with years of rot. It had a large nest of twigs and grass centered at the top of the tree which was about fifteen feet above the water. "This is where an Ospreys nests with her young," Rebecca said as she nodded up to the top of the tree.

There was nothing moving in the nest or, as a matter of fact, in the whole marshy area except the water itself as it lapped rhythmically against the fiber glass Jet Ski's—no visible Osprey, or her young, or even of any kind of bird in the marsh was to be seen. Steve and Nelly didn't even hear a single tree frog, or cricket, or any mystical marsh animal noises—nothing. There was just stillness.

Rebecca, thinking she could sense disappointment, tried to console her new customers by saying, "Some days we have good days for seeing the wild life and others days they seem to be uncooperative. 'Yesterday one of my groups was lucky enough to see an alligator consume a wild hog along the bank further down the river."

"We're from the city and I'm just in awe at not hearing or seeing anything at all. 'It's so peaceful and quiet out here." Steve didn't want to console Rebecca for lacking as a tour guide but truly wanted to share his comments on the peace and quiet of being away from manmade objects and being close to God's natural plan.

Rebecca looked relieved as Nelly agreed with Steve. Nelly thought that anyway she wouldn't take pleasure in seeing one animal consuming another like afore mentioned alligator consuming the wild boar.

They started the motors and buzzed loudly on down the river at a faster clip, looking from side to side for alligators, until Rebecca held her hand up to signal for them to stop again.

As she waved her hand across the water she said, "You can't see them but in this area the alligators are all probably underneath us. 'In the afternoon when the weather becomes hot they tend to stay under the river in the mud." Instinctually Nelly tucked her feet closer to the Jet Ski in a subconscious effort of keeping the alligators from jumping through the surface and snatching her feet. She hated to admit it but being amongst alligators, even if you couldn't see them, made her nervous as hell. Even though, being from sticks of *Montana* she was born into nature, swamp nature made her feel very much more vulnerable and nervous. The little Jet Ski just didn't seem like enough protection. She had been on the *Montana* lakes many times in her dad's homemade kayaks but there she had nothing dangerous under her, just North American Rainbow Trout and they were good to eat.

Nelly looked around at the peaceful spread of the river, still quiet and still without sound. If she didn't know that it was filled with alligators, she would want to sit here for hours communing nature, but right now she just wanted to move on down the river. A stork flew overhead casting an interesting reflection or shadowy figure on the water, Nelly couldn't guess.

Rebecca started her nature speech again, "Well go further down the river to a small cove where a sixteen foot alligator named Ole Charlie lives. 'He is one of the biggest Alligators in the swamp."Maybe he is in the mood for a visit today and for showing himself off while basking in the sun."

Rebecca turned on her Jet Ski again and again she raised her hand in a signal for the two of them to follow. Nelly remembered that she had forgotten sunscreen when she saw how pink her arms were becoming but decided it didn't matter; she was on an adventure.

Steve was second in line after Rebecca and seemed to be into nature as he sped along. Unlike Nelly, Steve seemed a natural to negotiating the little Jet Ski. By this time he caught on to the nuances and small tricks of working the quick turns. Nelly still felt awkward and clumsy. She felt very aware that they were in the same waters as huge carnivores—she tried to be a sport. Nelly was suddenly impressed with Rebecca at doing this every day.

They stopped yet again but this time at the edge of a narrow neck of a small cove circled by tall grassy banks.

Again with more instructions Rebecca explained, "It is very important to gun your engine in turning tightly through neck of the cove. 'There is only room for one Jet Ski at a time. 'Go into the cove and stop in the center. 'We'll sit quietly for a few minutes to see of Charlie will show himself."

To Nelly the center appeared only ten feet away from the embankment. It was going to be a tight fit.

Rebecca and Steve navigated the neck beautifully but Nelly, going too slow, banged loudly into the thick root structure of the embankment. Rebecca looked back in a panic at Nelly in hopes that she didn't damage the Jet Ski and had to piggyback with one of the others. This was the most dangerous part of the tour, even though she had never had any problems before. To her relief, the tough little Jet Ski bounced into the cove undamaged.

"I'm sorry," was all Nelly could say while her face turned red.

They pulled into the middle of the cove and Nelly excitedly pointed at the edge of the water where several miniature juvenile alligators, who were perfectly formed versions of their mother, sat at the water's edge—they were coming out of the grassy area with the intent of testing there young skills in the water. It was like a P.B.S. documentary on the hatching of alligators. "Do you think that Ole Charlie may be a girl?" Nelly asked in enlightenment. "There are some baby alligators over there at the edge," she continued as she realized that she was the only one of the three to notice right away and she drew everyone's attentions to the bank just a few feet away from them. "Aren't they cute!" she said so loudly that her voice echoed throughout the marsh.

Awakened by the sound, an ancient hidden monster reared up on scaly legs to veer at the tourists from behind a tall grassy mound just a few feet up the embankment. Its giant reptilian head supported wide open jaws revealing a mouth full of jagged teeth; a loud hissing sound came from somewhere deep within its smooth, slimy, meaty, throat—then while on all four of its disproportionate legs it rushed its large scaly torso down the embankment and into the cove creating a small canyon of water that rocked the Jet Skis violently.

"I don't want anyone to panic but ladies and gentlemen start your engines and get the hell out of here," Rebecca said as calmly as possible while already in motion. In a flash Rebecca and Steve sped safely out of the cove properly gunning the engine through the narrow neck and skidding around the bend in a sportsmen's text book turn of perfection—both motivated by an adrenaline rush inbreeded since caveman times. It's the either eat or be eaten mentality. They sped down the river a ways before realizing that Nelly wasn't behind them. When they back tracked, they found Nelly still sitting frozen stiff in the middle of the cove with Charlie being nowhere to be found.

"What do I do, my Jet Ski stalled?" Nellie asked quietly in a whisper as not to challenge the fact that she was still alive. "I think Ole Charlie is under me and my Jet Ski smells like it's flooded with gas—it won't start."

Steve looked in horror as he could make out the shadowy figure of Ole Charlie's body sitting at the bottom of the shallow cove just exactly beneath Nelly—it was as if Charlie was waiting for her to make the first move. He asked Rebecca, "Can Charlie knock her off the jet Ski?"

"Alligators have been known to knock over large canoes and can wait patiently under water for hours," she said with her mind in a whirl. "Nelly, stay quiet for a minute to see if Charlie will go back to the nesting area." Rebecca reached down and grabbed her bottle of water hanging off of the side and threw it over to the bank where the babies scurried about hoping to appeal to Charlie's motherly instincts and draw her off. Charlie almost took the bait and stirred the water up in a turn to face the other direction; however, she stayed put.

"I'll go in there and pull Nelly out," Steve started to move forward but Rebecca stopped him.

"Ole Charlie there is faster than you are and you could get the both of you killed," Rebecca said wisely. "My guess is that she, and we will probably need to call her Charlotte from now on, is just trying to protect her young. 'That makes her doubly dangerous."

The three of them sat there for ten minutes waiting for Old Charlie, or Charlotte now, to lose interest. Nelly slowly rubbed some sweat from her eyes and made a decision to try to outrun her. She didn't want to die of all deaths of being eaten by an alligator, what her husband David would think. She smiled at herself at being worried about David at a time like this, it was typical of her. She'd thought that she'd try the engine again: if it was same as in a car becoming flooded the answer was to wait until the gas had gone out of the carburetor. The gas should have gone out of the carburetor by now. All three of them held their breath as the she turned engine. It seemed like it was going to start but then sputtered and quit. Charlie still sat motionless. She tried the engine once more but this time it purred into motion and leaped forward; however, Nelly wasn't expecting the momentum and fell off the back of the Jet Ski into the waters right on top of the sixteen foot alligator. In a giant splendor rarely seen Charlie/Charlotte heaved ten feet of her sixteen foot frame straight out of the water landing on top of the Jet Ski. In the confusion Charlie grabbed the leather seat of the ski in her giant jaws and shook her head violently, pulling the seat from the ski. Realizing it wasn't flesh she let the seat go and twisted and turned looking for her prey.

Rebecca and Steve watched in frozen horror as their friend, and customer, seemed to have disappeared under the largest known alligator in the marsh. They sat helplessly studying the waters for a sign of Nelly, hoping in all hopes of a miracle that she survived the attack. Ole' Charlie seemed to be wondering where Nelly was too as she skirted her long scaly body easily from one end of the small cove to the other, in a grid like search. Minutes seemed to tick away. Because of the wet conditions, Rebecca and Steve didn't bring cell phones to call for help; it was up to them to find Nelly but how without endangering themselves too. They looked at each other for ideas but neither of them had any? Finally Charlie seemed to give up and swam, and then crawled, back to her nest on the top of the bank. Rebecca and Steve watched like two centennials toward the water for a long time for what they were sure was the body of Nelly. Could she have survived a ton of alligator falling on top of her?

"What shall we do," Rebecca asked Steve.

"You're the freak'n guide, you tell me," Steve's voice loudly echoed across the river stirring up a few birds.

"We'd better go back for help," Rebecca looked distraught and then seemed to be going into shock. "I've never lost a tourist before, never, never, never," she said as she started to cry.

Steve softened his tone, "Nelly's obviously gone and there is nothing we can do here. 'Let's go to one of the houses along the river and get someone to call 911." He lost Nelly and he didn't want to lose Rebecca to shock. She was white as a sheet. He led the way in what seemed to be like hours down the river to the nearest mansion and called out for help to an elderly lady trimming her garden. "Hey lady we need you to call 911…please! We lost our friend to an alligator. Can you take Rebecca here and bring her in your house until the police come? I think that she is in shock."

The elderly lady's thick shock of white hair whisked in the breeze she created as she ran to the river's edge. She pulled a cell phone from her pocket and gave it to Steve, then tugged Rebecca up on the grass. She pulled her sweater off and put it around Rebecca's shoulders as Rebecca sun kissed skin turn white.

Steve dialed the number but it took some time to explain where they were and that this was a little more involved than simply driving down a road to rescue them. They would need rescue workers, boats and an alligator expert.

When Steve was finished he handed the phone back to the white headed lady and asked, "What's your name mam?"

"Jackie…Jackie McLeod and I'm glad to help, my husband says I have an emergency at least once a year."

Steve looked at her kindly face and thought what an odd thing to say, she must be going senile. He was shocked by the unusually large and sky blue eyes of the elderly lady.

Back in the cove Nelly laid motionlessly packed in mud on the bank near the juvenile alligators. She was too unconscious to know that the babies had been crawling all over her for at least an hour. They seemed to not notice her packed in the mud or either weren't interested as they scooted over her to get to the water. She was unconscious and didn't wake up for at least an hour. Finally she fought her way to consciousness and sat up quickly with a sucking sound coming from her slimy bed. She drew a huge breath of air as if she was waking up from the dead. Her eyes looked like two white holes in a sea of mud like someone camouflaging themselves before the onslaught of jungle warfare, or hiding from an ominous enemy. Shaking loose of the mud she stood up and suddenly remembered where she was. She looked around fearfully to find Old Charlotte nowhere to be found, thank goodness. Nelly didn't know that being disappointed in her getting away, Charlotte had gone off hunting in another direction. The Jet Ski sat seat-free and motionless in the water at the embankment edge. As she attempted to stand she checked her body for injuries and found none, except a nasty bump on the head where the Jet Ski hit her as she was being thrown.

One of the babies tried to take a chunk out of her ankle and she pushed it off. "I say boy, don't you want a nice delicious wild hog like your mother," she mimicked the drawl of an old southern gentleman again. She was too relieved to be alive to think of anything else but getting the hell away from there.

She wondered how long she had been out and where were Rebecca and Steve? Had they left her there to be eaten by Old Charlie…she was angry with them? Then she remembered that she was invisibly buried in mud and maybe they thought that she had drowned and was at the bottom of the cove. Nelly remembered being thrown clear but that was all she remembered, if she knew that she was buried by a smaller alligator for a later meal she would have been horrified. She washed the mud from her arms and looked around for an escape plan. The only way out was back the way she came. The seat to the Jet Ski was on the bank five feet from her so she went and picked the shredded seat up and balanced it back on the Jet Ski. She managed to crawl on the wobbly seat and turned the on the engine. The little Jet Ski started up like a sewing machine. "Now why didn't you do that when I tried to start you the first time: you had to be attacked by an alligator before you would start," she said out loud. Then she asked the little Jet Ski, as if it was alive, "Scared shitless were you? I understand so was I?"

She knew her way back. Even though she was supposed to gun it through the neck of the cove she went through slowly again, using ser feet to keep her from banging against the bank. She'd do it her way this time.

While heading back she thought, Steve has a lot of explaining to do. While passing the mansions from the other side of the river she saw several Coastguard boats, a helicopter on pontoons and an elderly lady standing on a nearby dock. Nelly lifted her hand and waved at the elderly lady while wondering what that was all about? She started to go over and ask them but then thought she'd better get back to the other side of the bay and let Rebecca and Steve know that she was Ok. Ms. Jackie waved back and reached down to touched Steve's shoulder as he sat next to Rebecca in the grass.

"That's curious, I've never seen anyone go into the swampy marsh by themselves before, can you imagine that," Ms. Jackie said as Steve watched the lone skier glide slowly down the river.

"She looks covered in mud."

The river had washed some of the mud from Nelly's white shorts and Steve recognized them. He busted out laughing and the rest of them looked at him as if he was too far gone with grief and lost his mind. He threw his blankets off and ran yelling to remount his jet ski, "Call the search off, I've found the precious idiot."

"What did he say? One of the coastguard's searchers called up to Jackie. "He said that he found her, apparently that little muddy lady on the beat up Jet Ski is the woman that was eaten by the alligator."

"Hey, Nelly over here!!" Steve sped up his jet ski as he called to her but the noise was too loud.

He managed to get in front Nelly and used Rebecca's signal to stop the ski.

"I was trying to head back in a hurry so we could make the seaplane ride," she explained through mud caked lips.

He laughed and pulled her off her Jet Ski with his massive muscular arms and tucked her in front of him on his Jet Ski. The seat of her Jet Ski fell out into the water.

"Oh for heaven's sake, you'd think that I died or something," she laughed now catching on the whole situation without needing an explanation, "Is all that for me?"

"Yes," he admitted.

"Good Lord, look at the condition of the Jet Ski—it's a good thing I bought insurance on these," she shook her head.

"Silly girl, are YOU hurt anywhere?" he asked with his arm around her waist to balance her better while slowly guiding the Jet Ski the short distance back to the old mansion. Rebecca was standing up and cheering in the distance.

"My head hurts,—let's go back across the bay where there aren't any alligators, I never want to see another alligator as long as I live," she demanded.

"Anything you want, trouble maker, I have a personal escort over at that poor ladies house just for you," he said as he pointed toward the old two story brick mansion with flowers in the yard, the Coastguard boats sitting at the dock and the Bell helicopter on pontoons.

Suddenly she seemed worried, "Do you think that they will still let us take a seaplane ride, I'm a mess?"

Then he smirked and said, "You've got the whole ocean bay in which to bath."

"Now you sound like Rebecca."

CHAPTER 15

Nick Was Late With his Report

Nick called Mr. Durrell again. "Since yesterday, the subject seems to have gone on a little unplanned tour of the swampy marshes. 'It seems that we are at a place called the Boon Docks……..'" Nick rambled on about the Boon Docks.

"Thanks," Mr. Durrell's kindly voice came over the phone.

"Mr. Durrell, I'm going to call in my partner for a couple of days because I need a rest, his name is Mike. 'Plus, I'm worried about being spotted," Nick explained.

CHAPTER 16

At the Beach

Abby and Tracy had dropped Lillian off at her Grandmothers in a neighborhood of surprisingly of large old mansions lined with decretive gates, palm trees and well groomed flower gardens. It was unexpected but her Grandmother, a tiny frame of women fewer than five feet tall probably with the weight of a ten year old child and wearing a sarong, waited at the outside gate to greet them.

"Grandma seems to be psychic as she always knows when I come home," Lillian said in wonder.

Tracy and Abby could see where Lillian had gotten her bird bones, tiny arms and big dark eyes, features all women coveted.

"She's a cute little Granny," Tracy commented as she looked the elderly women over while thinking that the woman looked good for her age but probably didn't weigh more than eight-nine pounds.

Lillian rolled her eyes and said, "You don't know the half of it. Daa-dee-maa is a hand full but mostly I call her just Granny." Then she explained, "I've called the Inn and they are expecting you people, just drive down *Front Beach Road,* or the main drag and you'll see it plainly," Lillian gave instructions.

Abby and Tracy followed Lillian's directions to the Inn and found that the Inn staff treated the both of them like V.I.P. guests. They received side by side rooms on the first floor, one to accommodate Steve, both with sliding glass doors facing the ocean. The rooms were decorated with thick earth toned comforters on the bed and tan wall papered walls with soft patterns of peach colored seashells on the boarders. It smelled like sandal wood and fresh ocean spray. It was simple but classy. Tracy opened the doors to the beach and let the ocean breeze into the room. It picked up as set of off white shear curtains and lifted them in a soft gentle ballet. Abby stretched, yawned and then announced, "Great room but I'm going to take a nap."

While Abby slept, Tracy unloaded all their purchases from *Wal-Mart* into individual drawers to organize everyone. She noticed that Nelly had bought the *Junior Rock Band* shirts anyway, against their protests. She also noticed that Nelly had bought the thong panties she threatened them with so Tracy decided to sneak them in the trash. Nelly would never notice their disappearance. Tracy checked the bathroom for a hair dryer and was relieved to find one. She put Steve's bags on his bed in the adjoining room and then she stepped directly out onto the patio to look at the beach beyond. It was pure white like sugar, thus named "Sugar Sands." The ocean looked endless and the noise of sun bathers having a good time was like music to her ears. She had needed this type of relaxation for a long time.

She decided to stay instead of flying back to Atlanta. It was Friday, and nothing much so far had come out of her own pocket, just a few Wal-Mart clothes and a meal from *McMulligan's Bar and Grill,* so life was good. It was a free vacation. Nelly mentioned going to *Biloxi* and something about them having a free room waiting on them there; but she didn't give details of how this came about. Tracy thought that she could always borrow money from Abby or Nelly if she was short. She floated back into the room on cloud nine and chose the other Queen Size bed for a nap.

CHAPTER 17

The Sea Plane Ride

The small tour party finally arrived back at the *Fun-n-wet* dock via Coastguard. Much to Richard's surprise the ship was nearly the full length of the T-shaped dock and little larger than his prize Cessna. A young Coastguard officer unloaded Rebecca, Nelly and Steve on the dock and another assisted in tugging the Jet Skis over to their carrels. After Nelly signed a waiver toward not needing medical help, and after thanking their rescuers, the Coastguard ship went along its way through the bay—back to the ocean.

"What happened, I was about to come look for you," this time it was Richard's turn to be in shock. At five o'clock in the afternoon, they were two hours overdue. He was worried but never expected them to come back on a Coastguard ship.

"I'll explain in a minute, I need to get Nelly a change of clothes," Rebecca said as she pulled the hose out for Nelly to rinse off. Then she wondered up into the office and came out with some denim shorts and a *Fun-n-wet* T-shirt.

Steve felt sorry for Richard and explained swallowing hard at the thought of loosing Nelly, "Nelly ran into a fight with Old Charlie in the cove. 'We thought that she was a drowned but she was thrown clear—into the mud." Steve told Richard the whole story and they laughed at the ending.

"Nelly is a trouper, but I don't find it funny, it could have ended in disaster," Rebecca said still shaken up and then, as after she thought about it, started to giggle.

Richard looked at his wife lovingly and asked, "If you don't find it funny, then why are you laughing?"

Nelly stopped hosing herself down and contributed by saying, "It's not every day you practically get eaten by a giant alligator and escorted back by the Coastguard…I'd say we had a pretty good day so far. 'The question is, is anybody in the mood for a seaplane ride."

Richard couldn't believe that she could still be focused on a seaplane ride, "You bet Ms Nelly, Rebecca you go rest while I take these folks on their ride. 'Ms. Nelly would you mind drying off and changing your clothes while I'll warm up the plane?" He eyed the small women who had pulled her waist length hair out of a bun to let it fall for cleaning with the hose. Richard thought long hair was fine but he preferred women like Rebecca who kept their hair shoulder length and under control.

"Listen all, I'm sorry I cause such a commotion and ruined one of your Jet Ski's—do you think that the insurance will cover it?" Nelly was suddenly embarrassed.

****

It was glorious to be up so high and flying along the beach. The high-rises below looked like a toys and the ocean still looked endless. There were no words to describe the free feeling of flying far above everyone and being able to see every detail of the landscape, or seascape rather, all in one glance. Also, it was comforting to have nothing but ocean to soften a landing if they need to pre-land anywhere.

"Look, there is big fish following the boats," Nelly pointed out.

"In the clear greenish blue ocean at this height one can see the dolphins as they follow the boats," Richard explained. "I doubt if the people in the boats are even aware that the dolphins are following them."

"Wow this is cool," is all Steve had to say and kept repeating the same words over again as he looked out the window.

Nelly wondered how Richard was able to fly the little Cessna with his heavily arthritic hands but then she realized that it was like second nature to him, he was born to fly. He was the master of the sky and could fly with two legs in a cast and one arm in a sling.

They landed back into the bay and pulled up to the dock where Rebecca was ready with the key to the locker. Nelly took her phone out and called a sleepy Abby to come pick them up.

"We're ready and we're hungry if you want to grab a bit to eat?" Nelly asked Abby.

"I feel like pancakes, is the waffle house OK with you," Abby asked back.

"Sure!"

Nelly bought some post card pictures to help her with the precious memories, Rebecca hugged Nelly and then they all said their goodbyes to Richard. This was a day to remember for the two tour shop owners—and they hoped that they would never have another like it.

When Abby picked the two adventurers, Steve wanted to drive so he took over.

CHAPTER 18

Back in Montgomery Again

As Detective Dunwoody requested, David check into a hotel across the highway from The *Kumar Inn* where Nelly stayed, he took his shirt off and tried to take a nap; however, he couldn't sleep. The hotel had wireless capability so he put his lap top on the desk provided in each room and looked online for more bank transactions. He knew from the desk clerk at *The Kumar Inn* that the women were headed to *Panama City Beach* but he assumed that was all the information the desk clerk had, so he didn't ask. If he'd have asked, he'd known that they had gone down to stay at *The Kumar Inn Beach Resort* on the ocean but as it appeared there were no other bank charges. Little to his knowledge it took at least a day for the charges at *The Boon Dock* to catch up because they weren't connected through the internet, only by phone lines.

He'd let the police find her, he thought. That will teach her to run off without his permission. Instinct told David to put Nelly's little Browning hand gun in the hotel safe for safe keeping until in the morning when he planned on leaving. He placed the claim ticket in his wallet.

He decided to log into his work account to try to catch up with a couple of days work from remote access. He explained to his boss that he had a family emergency but he still didn't want to be fired so he arranged to take his work with him. Also, he thought that it would keep his mind off the bitch. His anger was starting to consume him. She was disrupting his life and costing them money in hotel bills, he was sure of it.

Working on the computer help a little to pass the time; however, around six O'clock that evening there was a knock on his hotel room door. When he peaked through the eyehole he saw Jack Dunwoody standing outside his door. Hoping that they had already heard something, he opened the door only to find, not one, but two Police officers outside. Beside the big out of shape detective he talked to earlier there was another tall blond Policeman.

"Mr. McMillan, this is Ed Stewart, the officer that detained your wife at the *Wal-Mart* parking lot last night," Jack introduced Ed.

"Why did you stop them inside the parking lot?" David asked actually irritated at the thought.

"Actually, *Wal-Mart* can get pretty dangerous at night, I was checking them out."

After Ed hung up the phone he had gone back to sleep. It would take time for Jack to ask the Judge to write out a warrant—and Ed had to work again that night so he wanted to stay fresh.

The two newly introduced men nodded at each other and then David asked, "Did you find her?"

"I've a search warrant for your car and hotel room, its routine," Jack Dunwoody said to immediately explain the situation head on.

"What the hell, I'm not a criminal," David said as he went over to put a shirt on over his nude chest which only gave his age away by a few grey hairs intermixed in a mass of black hair.

"I'm sorry Mr. McMillan, it's not personal but routine—after this we can concentrate on finding your wife. 'Ed here has been assigned by the chief to do whatever it takes to find your wife. 'The department feels some responsibility toward this because we did see her last night."

"OK, come on in and do what you must, just find my wife," David again acted the worried and willing to cooperate husband. He thought that this will make him look good to the police and Nelly look bad when they finally found her. David was all about image and getting everyone on his side. It made it easier to put Nelly in her place.

The two police officers found nothing after searching his hotel room and car. David was pleased with his own insightfulness as neither looked into his wallet for the claim ticket.

After leaving the room Jack asked Ed what he thought.

"I don't know," Ed said, "It just appears to me that he is a distraught husband; he may not be dangerous."

Jack's instincts were heightened, "I don't know Ed—something just seems to be out of place about all this."

Jack was the more experienced of the two and Ed had a great appreciation for his instincts. Jack had saved Ed and others many times with his knack for judging character and situations. Jack had an idea, "I have my granddaughter's birthday party tomorrow but would it be OK if I send you down to *Panama City Beach* to see if you can catch up with Nelly McMillan and interview her—I need her side of the story? 'I have a feeling that she is just down there having a good-ole-time for herself while her husband worries. 'It's probably going to turn out to be nothing but as you said before, we need to cross our t's."

Ed thought about it for a minute, "I have midnight duty this week."

Jack assured him, "I can fix that." Then Ed added, "I think that it's time they start promoting you to detective, I'm going to retire."

Ed was a little surprised at Jack's revelation, "You can't retire Jack—you aren't old enough."

Ed laughed, "Oh yes I am, and you know it—you fuck. You'll just have to finally step up to the plate to take a real man's responsibility."

"You old fart, now you're just hurting my feelings," Jack laughed.

CHAPTER 19

Friday Night at John's by the Sea

That Friday night, back at the hotel Nelly thought that it might be just one day away from the event of their suspension but it seemed like a lifetime to her. It all seemed so surreal that none of them had been home since work yesterday. Nelly took a shower and begged off for supper at the Waffle house; then opted for bed. She was sore and tired after their ordeal at *Fun-n-wet*. It was no typical day. A tinge of guilt raked her soul as she thought about calling David to let him know that she was alright but she was just too tired to face the music right now. On the other hand Steve was raring to go; he wanted to see the action on the "Red Neck Riviera" as was the reputation of *Panama City Beach*. In order to guard her reputation, Nelly decided not to sleep in Steve's room in the extra bed. Abby volunteered by saying, "no need in any of us doubling up when there is enough beds, so I'll go."

After ensuring that Nelly didn't need to be checked out by the local urgent care, Steve was ready to go. The other's knew a little about what went on but wondered to what extent. They hadn't been told the whole story yet. Steve promised he'd tell them at dinner.

Tracy and Abby were pleased to have Steve to themselves as Nelly had him all day. Instead of the waffle house they found a small bar and grill called *John's by the Sea*, located down *Front Beach Road* across from the Howard Johnson. There was a little known Blue Grass Band called the *Son's of an Ugly Wolf* playing near a small dance floor. Tracy, Abby and Steve found a table and ordered a beer each; then ordered a seafood dinner for four, Abby called it her treat. Soon a male attendant brought a platter of coconut fried shrimp, chicken fingers, fried calamari, fried scallops, fried flounder, fresh coleslaws and French fries. The attendant gave each of the three a refill of beer and a plate with the inscription of the restaurant above a pirate. A row of dipping sauces extended across the table. There was tartar sauce, mustard sauce, cocktail sauce, honey mustard sauce, horse radish sauce and chipotle sauce. Ravished by the long day, they all dove in with a healthy appetite. After eating their second seafood meal of the day they each finished it off by ordering a big chunk of key lime pie, which was recommended by the attendant when he claimed that it was the best in the south, made with actual true key limes. The attendant was right as it had just the right amount of fresh lime, sugar and whipped topping.

Satiated, the three of them had the attendant move their group out to one of the restaurants picnic tables on the deck facing the ocean. It was much cooler and they could hear the rushing waves. They could also see flying fish shimmering in the moon light as they hung for second's yards above the ocean's surface. The three of them chatted on while enjoying the fresh salty air. Tracy would have loved to have danced but Steve didn't seem interested. She wondered if he ever danced.

Then Abby asked, "How did your day go?"

Tracy and Abby listened with large eyes as Steve told the story of the alligator and the Coastguard.
"Wow!" was all the girls had to say. Tracy worried that Nelly might have hidden injuries from her ordeal but Steve assured her that she was OK and spontaneously sang a made up song to commemorate the ordeal.

Knowing that the ladies liked his music, he was confident to sing it for them. They laughed at his funny version, especially when he sang *"Ole Charlie turned out to be ole Charlotte."*

"You really should be a famous singer or something," Tracy complimented.

Nelly and Steve's adventure motivated Tracy to want to have adventures of her own as she suggested that they all go parasailing tomorrow. At first, taking tourist attractions didn't seem too adventuresome until they heard Steve and Nelly's story. Now it seemed exciting.

Steve agreed to go parasailing but Abby said she'd rather watch from the beach. They all knew Nelly would be game because she basically fit the description of a "live wire." She was game for everything, except the night life.

The three of them sat there until the wee hours of the morning laughing, talking and just generally have a good time.

"Steve, what animals do the three of us remind you off," Abby said surprisingly out of her usual no nonsense character.

"Nelly reminds me of a sort of a lion with that a head full of hair, Tracy I don't know what you remind me of but something spectacular and Abby you remind me of a little golden Labrador puppy."

Tracy seemed disappointed that Steve couldn't name an animal for her as she would really like to put a visual to her appearance. She would press him later.

They decided to go back to the room to sleep off their second round of seafood and booze for the day.

As they came out to little tan Cruiser parked in the sandy parking lot, Abby pointed across the empty lot to a black impala with darken windows. "I've seen that car several times before," she pointed out as she ran over to the window, cupped her hands against the glass to see if she could see anything inside.

"I wonder if anyone is inside?" she wondered out loud.

"Abby, you better get away from there…there maybe someone in there," Steve demanded while looking out for Abby's safety.

Inside the car Nick Barkowski was holding his breath as Abby pressed her nose against the glass just inches from his nose. If it wasn't for the tinted windows, Abby would have noticed that the only thing separating them was a thin layer of glass. For now, Nick wasn't sure what to do. Abby walked around the car to look at the license plate.

"Ummm, that's curious, they're from Atlanta too," she shrugged her shoulders.

"Come on Abby, I'm tired," Tracy yawned as she crawled into the Cruiser.

In the sedan, Nick let out his breath as they walked away. Had he been made? Perhaps it was time to put an end to this assignment. He'd sleep on it and in a bed tonight, he thought, not in the car. The car was beginning to smell funky.

CHAPTER 20

Tracy

"Where's your mom, I can't reach her," Daniel, Tracy's Ex, asked his stepson over the phone. Daniel was a barrel of a man with big meaty hands and the furry chest of a bear. His hair was snow white and he sported a beard.

"I don't know, I'm not Mom's keeper," Tom said with irritation. He didn't understand his parent's relationship. They had been divorced for years; Daniel already had new Girlfriend, so why do they keep in touch? It was annoying to always answer questions about each other to each other.

"Nancy and I want to go to Sea Island this weekend and I need someone to feed the dog," Daniel sounded frustrated at Tracy not answering her phone.

"She hasn't picked up her home phone for two days," Daniel complained.

"Try her cell phone," Tom suggested thinking that mom wasn't his servant so why did Daniel expect her to be there for him still after several years of being divorced.

Daniel had been a good father to him and Tom would like to see the two of them get back together but he didn't like being the go between. Tom didn't like that even now after the divorce, Daniel felt that he had the right to put Tracy to task. He used Tracy's love for him and her son didn't like it.

"Ok, I just thought that maybe you had some idea of what's going on with her," he said before hanging up without a goodbye.

He didn't know about Nancy, she had already started to complain about his eating habits where Tracy never complained. He didn't think that he wanted Tracy back after she left him but sometimes he wondered. Tracy made his life so much easier; however, Nancy had a college degree and money. In the divorce, Tracy had given up easily; he had gotten the house, the car and all of his savings without a battle, so what was it with her?

He'd just have to get to the bottom of this. After all he had done for her, and all she had put him through, she should at least answer the damn phone. He felt she owed it to him. He gave her a good life.

Daniel dialed Tracy's cell phone.

Nelly had a good night's sleep and, as a result, was up earlier than everybody else. She had brushed her teeth and combed out the tangles. Then just as she had decided to go to eat a continental breakfast, Tracy's phone rang.

"Hello," she answered.

"Tracy, is that you?" Daniel asked.

"Tracy is asleep, can I take a message?"

"This is her Ex-husband, Daniel, could you please wake her up, I need for her to feed the dog this weekend," Daniel's demand made Nelly testy.

"Tracy won't be able to feed your dog this weekend as she is in *Panama City Beach* and Monday we'll be in *Biloxi*, Nelly said with satisfaction.

"Ah, Ok, you all have fun," he said as he hung up the phone.

Nelly hangs up with Daniel while issuing the expletive, "you ass hole!"

After talking with Tracy's Ex, Nelly felt a little nudge of guilt because she hadn't told the girls that she was planning on taking a proposition from a complete stranger for their hotel room in *Biloxi*. They'd probably would have a cow if they knew it was from one of the drunk men at the bar Thursday night. It was one thing to have drinks and laughs with strangers but quite another to traipse off to *Biloxi* with him. Well, she didn't lie; they just hadn't asked how she had a free room waiting on them. Nelly suddenly thought of David, how was he going to take it?

After hanging up, Daniel wondered what was going on. Tracy never told him of any vacation coming up on her schedule. She always told everyone where she was.

CHAPTER 21

Nick's Spiritual Experience

At seven a.m. Saturday morning Lillian started her daily shift behind a long counter facing the hotel lobby of *The Kumar Inn Beach Resort*. The lobby could best be described as a large opened mall, with a green leafy patterned carpet, made solely for the utilitarian purpose of providing comfort to many tourists and guests as they cut through the building to the ocean. One side of the lobby was a wall of glass facing the ocean and the other side of the lobby was a store front to a small gift shop packed full of beach paraphernalia. There was a wide open corner room with a counter top filled with mounds of sweet rolls, boiled eggs and beagles and light green round tables randomly scattered around awaiting the occupation of hungry guests looking for more than ample delicious continental breakfast. The aroma of Idaho's waffle iron drifted through the lobby as she cooked the hotels signature blueberry waffles that attracted many guests.

Lillian's uncle liked to hire retired persons who lived in nearby trailer parks to work for him. He thought that they were more reliable than the usual college students hired by most of the other hotels along the beach front. First there was the sweet natured retired lady named after the state of Idaho, tanned to rawhide, who managed the breakfast bar for the last five years—she especially loved to cook waffles for the children. Then there was the retired couple he hired last year whose jobs were to clean the lobby and pool areas of debris and cigarette butts. The couple usually carried small dust pans and brooms but this early in the morning they pushed vacuum cleaners. They were all once a part of the baby boomers raising typical families in typical suburban homes near typically large cities; being typical housewives and typical office workers. Now they were living their life's dream of moving to the warmer climates of the Florida Gulf Coast to perform atypical jobs working in hotels on the Gulf beach to supplement their retirement and enjoy the sun. Lillian smiled at the elderly woman vacuuming as she raised her snowy covered head and smiled back. Regardless, Lillian's uncle only hired family members to run the desk and the accounting department. She couldn't figure in her mind if it was because he was supporting family members with good jobs or if it was because he only wanted people he could trust close to the money, maybe for both reasons.

As Lillian begun restocking the brochures she thought how much she identified with the elderly employees. Working at a hotel right on the beach was a positive experience made possible by an atmosphere of lively vacationers having fun. Then Lillian's thoughts went to her four new friends. She hoped that they enjoyed their room last night and wondered if they would stay long—or would they go soon to *Biloxi, Mississippi* as they planned? It was kind of vague but Nelly said that they would stay free, although Nelly didn't really explain to anyone how they had a free room. However, Lillian hoped that they would stay as she had grown to like the three ladies. They were fun and pleasant to be around.

At eight a.m. the lobby started to fill up with waking customers. Lillian wondered what the day in the lobby would look like with time lapse photography over twenty-four hours. First it would be herself and the cleaning people, then a steady stream of people in colorful beachwear going in all directions, then back to another lone desk clerk in the night.

While helping customers with directions to a gift shop with a shark pool down the street, Lillian spotted Nelly McMillan coming through the lobby on her way toward the breakfast.

"Lillian, it's good to see you," Nelly waved and yelled over the noises.
"Hi, Ms. Nelly…how did you people sleep last night? Did you like your room?" she said in her usual attractive India accent as Nelly neared.

"Oh, Lillian the room is wonderful…much more than I expected," Nelly was genuinely glad to be able to thank Lillian. "Thank you so much!"

"My uncle was more than happy to repay you for your kindness of driving me here safely," Lillian said modestly. "My uncle wants you people to come dine with us in our private dining room tonight to thank you for himself."

Nelly wasn't expecting that but graciously accepted—then went on her way to the breakfast room for a continental breakfast.

Nick Barkowski also crossed the lobby that Saturday morning on his way for a swim. Last night he decided that he'd been cooped up in the car far too long and, as a result, checked into the hotel for good night's sleep. He had miscalculated last night and may have even been "made" by the short haired lady named Abby. He was certain that the subject for which he was following was not going anywhere for now and he felt that he needed to get some rest and exercise. Earlier that morning he left a message for his secretary to have another investigator sent to relieve him for a day or two. The office wasn't open but he was sure that his secretary would return his message soon. He wanted Mike Coffer, an investigator who worked for Nick on part-time bases to fly a small carrier to *Panama City Beach*. He was hoping Mike could find a different colored rental car with the same tinted windows. Nick thought about the lady named Abby who was almost nose to nose with him through the window of his Impala. He grinned at the incident and chuckled out loud drawing the attention of a young teenage boy with red hair and glowing white skin. Now the incident was funny but last night it didn't seem so funny.

Earlier Nick had stopped by the gift shop to buy a swimsuit and a tooth brush; he felt it was safe to take a couple hours of sleep and then to take advantage of a swim in the ocean, all at his client's expense. The Cruiser was still in the hotel parking lot and judging by the hour that he guessed that the subject went to bed, he supposed that everyone would be sleeping right now.

He noticed that the young female that they had picked up in *Montgomery, Alabama* was working behind the desk. Lillian looked up at the same time that he was studying her but Lillian's modestly prevailed as she averted her eyes. Nick thought that Lillian was very beautiful. Under different circumstances, he thought how much he'd enjoy getting to know her. Something about Lillian reminded him of his deceased wife.

Nick's child looked like his wife. He felt a ting of pain while remembering his child and the hard decision he made to give her up. The Native Americans do things differently and his mother, being a full Native American princess, listened to the tribunal decisions. When his wife, Red Feather died, the tribal council met and decided that the child would be better off in a home with two parents—Nick's mother agreed with the council. They came to him and told him that the spirit of his wife would be happier if he would give up Star to a young childless Native American couple. It was painful but probably a wise decision because his child was being raised on a large ranch as an only child—admired and loved by many human and animal friends. As their only adopted daughter, she would not only inherit the couple's name but their vast estate which included interests in the only casino on the reservation. As his child Star would only inherit his sadness toward losing her mother and a disappointed grandmother when he gave up medicine.

Nick, known to his daughter as an uncle, looked forward to seeing her at family parties and at her many equestrian competitions. Star was natural on a horse.

A CHANGE OF LUCK

Back to reality, swimming was the way he earned his way through college and he still loved it. As he continued on through the lobby, he was fully unaware of all the females taking notice of his perfectly shaped, naturedly smooth, hairless and lean body. It wasn't overly muscular: only tall and graceful like an old time warrior, only in Hawaiian style swim trunks. Without the modern swimsuit he would have looked like he came from a *Charles Russell* painting. His long black hair was loose down his back. Once outside the double doors leading to the beach, he took a deep breath and then ran toward where endless the sky met the endless ocean—he ran like a wild Cheyenne into *The Battle of the Little Bighorn* before diving into a large oncoming wave.

As he came out of the other side of the wave, he heard shouts coming from the shore from the same red headed teenage boy he saw earlier; he was waving and pointing past his direction to the Ocean beyond. Nick turned around to look behind him and saw young women on float about thirty-foot further out. She seemed to be oblivious to the blacked tipped fin circling her as she lay on an air mattress with her eyes closed; her sun baked body was stuffed in a floral bikini and the tips of her blond hair fanned out floating in the ocean. At first, Nick wondered if the fin was real, or was it just a dolphin, or possibly a joke.

"Hey, Lady wake up," he hollered with his hands cupped around his mouth but she didn't open her eyes.

Then terror struck in Nick's heart as the rubbery grey nose and jaw of a shark revealed itself from between waves. Its jaws opened wide to reveal razor sharp teeth in the totality of their destructive capability. Its dark soulless eye seems to be looking toward Nick when it suddenly flipped down its white protective sheath revealing its intent to attack by protecting its eyes. Seconds seemed like minutes as Nick wandered what to do. The sharks mindless feeding frenzy was about to begin. It was nature in its purist most evil form.

It was like a frightening frame by frame horror movie as the waves lifted up to hide and then to reveal each frame of the attack. First there was the shark and then there was the blood spewing out into the ocean, coloring the ocean red. By now the woman was screaming and thrashing desperately trying to get away. Nick swam like a mad man without regard for his own safety toward the women. He hoped he wasn't too late to save her; blood was turning the ocean red all around her.

After reaching the women he literally tried to pull her from the jaws of the shark, but the beast would not let go. Although he was half white, he heard the music of his Native American Ancestor sing out to encourage him. He didn't question his sanity in hearing their voices as his mother had told him that he would at some point in his life. You can fight the spirit of the beast, they sang. Let your soul reach the spirit of the beast and ask him to give up his evilness—to let the women go back to her family.

Something deep within his body gave him unnatural courage and strength; his strength was even with strength of the shark as they both wrestled for the woman's life, one to save the women and other to cause her demise. Nick's voice seemed disembodied as he croaked out in a crazy frenzy to follow his ancestors instructions, "Go find another meal today, great beast; this one is not for you."

The eyes of the grey shark rolled over white again as it thrashed even more to pull at its next meal. Nick's plea to the spirit of the beast did not work. Again, he heard the voices of his forefathers singing, giving him more confidence, encouraging him not to give up, as yet again they instructed Nick to ask the beast to let the women go back to her family.

He kicked out harder at the beast's nose and yelled, "Go find a big fish to eat and let the women's flesh go."

Again, without regard to his own safety, he pulled with all his might at the women while, at the same time, fearing he would do more damage. The shark let go as if it understand Nick's plea; then the shark flipped its powerful tail to swim away. Nick pulled the ashened colored woman to his smooth chest with one large arm and swam back to shore with the other. When he pulled her up on the sand, her thigh looked like a piece of torn meat with tendons and broken veins spidering out in different all directions—the wound was so deep that the bone was exposed.

"Call 911," he called out to the gathering crowd, "and someone bring me a big roll of Saran Wrap."

He felt for her pulse and was relieved to find one. As for injured women, she was only at herself enough to think that she had seen an angel and she would always remember the color of the angel's eyes, one blue and one brown.

Inside the lobby, an out of breath red headed teenage boy ran up to the desk and yelled excitedly to Lillian, "Shark bite—get Saran Wrap."

"Wait, slow down," she said as she heard the urgency in his voice. .

"I said get Saran Wrap for a guy fix'n a shark bit... please hurry lady...she is bleeding to death," his voice was loud and filled with panic.

She ran to the breakfast room and, to the surprise of those enjoying their breakfast, pulled a huge roll Saran Wrap off of the dispenser; and then followed the skinny red headed teenager out to the beach where they found a bathing suit clad crowd gathered. There, the handsome Native American gentleman Lillian saw in the lobby earlier was crouched over young a woman who had her quad muscle completely torn loose from her left thigh. Lillian almost fainted at the sickening site. Nick grabbed the wrap from Lillian's hand. Then lifting the leg expertly by the distal end, the foot, raised the leg high enough to administer the rapping to the injured thigh. He handed the injured woman's heel to Lillian to hold so he could use both hands. As if she was a natural, Lillian followed his direction without question.

"There will probably be some sand contamination of the wound but the Saran Wrap will act like a skin in helping the blood to reabsorb back into the body so there will be less blood loss." Nick didn't know who he was explaining this to but Lillian seemed to understand the concept anyway.

"No major arteries have been torn, so she should make it," he continued.

Soon the sound of an ambulance echoed in the distance; then there were paramedics pushing the crowd aside. Three paramedics heaved the women on a heavy wooden body board with handles on each end, they taped her head down with orange tape and then started an IV of ringers lactate to replace the fluids that she had lost; and then they used a syringe to administer pain medication through a fresh I.V., possible morphine. One of the paramedics saw the Saran Wrapping on the leg and understood its purpose. He commented that someone on the beach really knew their first aide. He commented correctly when he said that this action probably saved the young woman's life but Nick hoped it also saved her leg.

After the ambulance left and the crowd dissipated, a blood covered, badly shaken Nick staggered into the gulf and sunk into the water. As he dropped to his knees to wash the blood from his arms and legs in the salty water, Lillian came up behind him.

"Sir, what you people did was brave," she complimented him in her sweet accented voice.

He looked blankly into her lovely face before he remembered who she was.

"Come inside and I'll fix you some hot tea," she coaxed, "I'll also see to it that you receive some hot breakfast or a sandwich...or whatever you people want to eat."

"No, I'll be OK," he said as he rose from the imported sugar white sand and brushed off his knees. Then his face softens as he saw genuine concern on Lillian's pretty face.

"I'm Nick, call me Nick," he repeated himself as he ran his hands through his dark hair.

The name Nick just didn't seem to fit, Lillian thought. He was obviously Native American and a beautiful specimen at that. However her entire family was from India and none of their names fit either.

Lillian insisted, "Its hotel policy to help the customers, please come let me ask Idaho to get you some breakfast or at least some tea. Oh, and my name is Lillian Kumar"

After some insisting, Nick followed Lillian inside. As they entered the building, Nick thought about all that had happened and about what seemed to be the spirit of his ancestors helping him by encouraging him to fight the shark. Or was he imagining it? He never believed in an unassisted drug induced chat with ones ancestors like the traditionalists of his tribe. However, something happened out there in the ocean—something spiritual. Could his mother be right in that someday he would hear the spirit of his ancestors call to him—then to receive his Native American name from the living creatures of the earth? It seemed hardly believable but something real did happen out there.

Inside there were guests waiting for help at the desk but Lillian excused herself for a moment to get Nick to the kitchen.

"Please make him some tea with lemon, Idaho," Lillian asked politely, "I'll be back immediately after I help the other guests."

While sitting behind the counter, Nick looked up to see a curious Nelly staring back at him. "Oh God in heaven," he said at a taken back

Idaho, "Now I've really blown it." Idaho didn't question him but made him a waffle instead.

As Nick waited for his breakfast he thought about his job. Mr. Durrell will have to trust Nick's decision to let Mike take over for a couple of days. It's always better to work as a team; plus he wanted to have a chance to stay in the hotel for a couple of days to rest. He wondered who Lillian was and how she was related to the case; it was a good excuse to explore the possibilities and perhaps get to know her better.

CHAPTER 22

The Finding

Before leaving the dining area, Nelly wrapped one more jelly roll in a napkin and refilled the paper coffee cup. She wanted to finish breakfast while overlooking the ocean. She also wanted to find a private place to make several phone calls from her old Samsun cell phone. Nelly decided not to use the blue tooth because the breeze would cause a dull roar in the speaker. She had in mind to take up John's offer of a free room at the *Belle Rose Casino* but she was nervous. She wasn't sure it was a good idea because he was in essence a stranger whom she only just met. What if he was a conman, or a rapist, or worse—a murderer? She had seen these scenarios on the news reports where unsuspecting women had gotten into a mess with strangers. Well she would take a chance.

As she walked out the antebellum style front doors of the resort hotel, she noticed a van with a CBS news sign on the side of it. A camera crew was taping an interview with a teenage boy with the reddest hair and the whitest skin that she had ever seen. She knew something went on with a shark bite this morning but wasn't expecting to walk right into the interview as she left the building. Embarrassed at interrupting the session, she hurried past the door to get out of direct line of the camera. The camera man had a gift for visually interesting photography so he decided to catch this bystander as she shot behind the boy. To the cameraman Nelly looked like lady Godiva with her hair draped loosely over her shoulder, hanging nearly to her waist. It was a rare glimpse of beautiful older women still in her natural state of having long hair. Her large eyes seemed to look coyly toward the camera as they glanced in apology for the interruption; it was an attractive moment caught on film—then back to the boy.

Nelly walk down the beach until she found an abandoned cement bench with broken seashells embedded in the dried mortar. Deciding that this was as good as any place to make a phone call, she sat down on her ruff perch and found John's number in her contact list.

"Well, who the hell is this," John's gruff voice startles her over the phone.

"Um, my name is Nelly, you met me at the Bar and Grill across from the *Hillcrest Grand Garden Inn* in Atlanta Thursday night," she said flustered, nervous and shy, all at the same time.

"Oh… yeah, girl, where ya'll been, where are ya now?" his voice sounded genuinely excited to hear from her.

"We took your suggestion and went to Florida, we're in *Panama City Beach*," she said with new found confidence.

"You still have a room in *Biloxi* for us at the *Belle Rose Casino*?"

"What day is this…oh yeah Saturday? I've been so busy getting my business matters straight before we head down from to *Biloxi* that I've lost tract of my days but I was hope'n that you'd call," he sounded sincere.

"I'll tell you what, I hadn't planned on being there till Monday but I'll come on Sunday night and meet you at the hotel bar at Midnight. I'll have Heather, my recreationalist at the store, call the hotel and have a room ready for ya'll tomorrow evening after 3:00 p.m. 'Does that sound good enough for ya, young lady?" His voice was so dynamic and powerful over the phone, like a man used to having his way. He also had a very heavy charming southern drawl.

Smiling at him calling her a young lady, Nelly thought that it might be fun putting their entertainment in the hands of a man who knew how to take charge. He sounded about as exciting and as dangerous as almost being eaten by old Charlie, or Charlotte.

"OK, we will look forward to it," she laughed. She received her instructions as to what to do when they reach the hotel before she hung up. The others probably didn't remember John's face so John instructed Nelly to play a joke on them by making them think that she was picking him up at the bar. Then she would explain where she had met him. He seemed harmless and just like a fun loving guy so Nelly decided to play along.

The breeze kept blowing her hair around so she pulled out a brush and an elastic band from rather large bag to style her hair in a rope braid. As she did this she admired the beach and watched the Para-Sailors over the ocean. She agreed to go Para Sailing with Steve but, in light of recent shark attack, she was apprehensive. Well, statistically it probably won't happen again so she thought that she would give it a try. The man that saved the women from the shark attack was a hero and the entire hotel was a buzz; however, he remained anonymous. She wondered if it was the Native American guy that Lillian was tending to in the breakfast area. It would make sense. She was hovering around him as if he was an important official from another country.

CHAPTER 23

Men Watch the News

On the national twelve-O-clock news all over the country four men applicable to the case happened to see Nelly's cameo on the television.

Ed was eating a hamburger plate at *The Blue Plate Restaurant* when a picture of Nelly's face flashed across the restaurants TV set. The subject of the interview was about a shark bite victim but it appeared that Nelly McMillan crossed behind the camera when it zeroed in on her. Ed was just an hour away from the *Panama City Beach* so he was confident that he could get his business done and return home in this evening. He polished off the last bite of hamburger and the last gulp of sweet tea, paid his bill and rushed out the door. He was supposed to leave earlier this morning but the unmarked car was held up for a couple of hours with another case.

He felt that he had to reach Nelly McMillan before her husband. Chances are he had seen the news too.

@#%&*****

Back in *Montgomery*, David is laying on his hotel bed watching the news when Nelly appeared full screen. "Alright bitch, I have you now," he says as he hurriedly packed his things. He retrieved the old antique browning from the hotel safe then found his rental car in the parking lot. He decided that he wasn't waiting any longer. Now that he knew where she was, he no longer needed the *Montgomery p*olice department to find her. On the road he called their son Neal again to make sure that Neal hadn't heard from her. He also wanted to make it clear to his son that what Nelly was doing to him was wrong. It was important to him that Neal was on his side.

Neal felt his phone vibrate in his overall pocket. He was in the middle of changing the oil on a Camaro and his hands were covered in grease. He pulled an oil soaked rag halfway hanging out of his front pocket and whiped his hands before answering the flip phone.

"Dad I'm in the middle of something here, can I call you back later?" he asked impatiently.

David wished that Neal could get a better job other than an auto mechanic. He loved his son and wanted what was best for him…besides it was embarrassing. Nelly kept telling everyone how proud she was of Neal for working so hard every day but Nelly was too hard on the child. She wouldn't let him quit, saying that he needed to pay his dues and that it was a part of life to go through tough times; that it built character. That was just crazy.

"I was just calling to see if you heard from your mom?"

"Dad, where are you?" Neal said worriedly. He knew his father well enough to know that his father had a penchant for the possessiveness and tendency to be out of control. However, after spending half his childhood in counseling Neal was finally able to place his father in a box that said "fragile handle with care."

"I'm on my way to *Panama City Beach* to drag you mother home, she has lost her mind," he proclaimed.

"Dad I agree that she shouldn't have taken off like that without telling someone—but again I'll encourage you to go home and wait for her, she'll come home," Neal begged.

Neal didn't know why but he suddenly felt the need to protect his mom from his dad. David had never raised a hand to her but he did have a confusing way of sending unspoken messages. Neal didn't like the message his father was sending now.

David hung up on Neal without saying anything else.

Neal crawled out of the oil changing bay and walked to the office. He had stayed out of his parents problems all his life but it was time to intervene. In the past, Neal's mom had protected him but now it was Neal's turn to protect her. He loved his dad but his dad could be a holy terror. Neal should know. His father knew how to push his limits and work under the subterfuge of being wonderful. To the casual onlooker David could seem like a loving and giving father, but away from the public eye, he was demanding, verbally abusive and critical of everything. Nelly succumbed to his demands, fed his ego and believed in the general opinion that she was the bad spouse—an illusion David purposely kept alive. Neal just wanted to see his parents happy.

"Roger I have a family emergency, I'm going to have to go" Neal was at a point that he didn't care if he was fired or not, the job was pretty heavy anyway.

"I don't really know when I'll be back."

"Does it have anything to do with your mom being in *Panama City Beach*?" his boss asked.

"How did you know where my mom was?" Neal was taken aback.

"She was on the noon news in front of *The Kumar Beach Resort Inn*, she's a pretty lady," Roger explained the news segment.

"I think that Dad is on a rampage," Neal said as he headed out to his street racing enhanced car with a large winged spoiler on the back. It was mostly for show.

#$@&888*****************

Daniel Malone, Tracy's Ex, also sees Tracy's friend and coworker on the TV. He couldn't understand why but it bothered him that Tracy didn't notify him of her plans to go to Florida. Even after their divorce they always told each other about upcoming events. They still shared in everything; the children's birthdays, holidays and the new grandson. Had she thrown twenty years away by separating from him or had he thrown twenty years away by jumping on the opportunity of divorcing her? Everything in their home reminded him of her. She planted yellow tulips in the backyard, hung the humming bird feeder in their window and picked the pink and black wallpaper in the kitchen. Was he still in love with her? Maybe it was time to find out…before it was too late. He especially remembered her love for chimes…he hated chimes then but now he would give anything to hear her chimes ring again on the patio; also, to smell the cinnamon and apple aroma from one of her burning candles. He missed her. That was several years ago but he still loved her. He decided that he was going to tell her.

#$@&99999***********

William Durrell catches Nelly on the noon news. "Allison Dear, can you make reservations for me on the next Commercial flying out of Casper Wyoming," he asks his wife.

Her eyes brighten, "So you're finally going after her?" When their son Bill Jr. died in the rodeo accident last year Allison thought that it would be the death of Bill, until he was told he had another child. Jason had never married and they had no grandchildren in which to leave the family estate. It had been in the family for generations and Bill wanted to pass the estate down to his own flesh and blood, as his father had before him.

William had taken the family money made on a ranch near *Nashua, Montana*, moved to *Casper, Wyoming* and then bought an oil well. He sold the oil well and built stores, car dealerships and even packing plants that specialized in Elk meat all over *Montana* and *Wyoming*; all the while maintaining the old family home place. However, all that he worked for seemed useless when his son died, he seemed without an heir. Then he heard from her. Back in the early sixties she was the wildest thing he'd ever met and he indulged her fancies. She would have been jail bait now-a-days but back then times were different. Next thing he knew she had married his best friend and so Bill had to move on with his life, he had forgotten about her until six months ago, when he ran into her on a business trip in *Portland, Oregon*. She had heard that he was in town and was sitting at the bar of his hotel debating rather to call his room or not when, as fate would have it, he sat down next to her.

She was much older but had the same recognizable features as when she was a teenager, so he recognized her right away. They talked about Nashua and old school friends. They talked about her husband, who at one time was his best friend. At a bar she asked him if he had any children and he sadly told her the story of his son's death. He guessed that she felt sorry for him and that is was why she finally confessed. She told him that she and her husband had raised six children but that she had never told her husband that the first child was not his. Her husband died last year never knowing and she could hardly bear the guilt of the secret anymore.

"The child was your child. 'I had to tell someone to set this all right. I never told my husband and I should have told him the truth but I loved him too much to hurt him," Maria burst out into tears as Bill tried to grasp the meaning of all this.

He held her as she cried letting all the guilt rush out of her so she could finally forgive herself. He knew that she was troubled but he was elated, he had another child, a female child. He kissed his old girlfriend on the forehead and said, "May God bless you, it's the sweetest news I've ever heard!"

"What are you going to do?" she pleaded with him.

"Where is she?" he asked.

"She is down in Atlanta, Georgia. 'She married young and we haven't had much contact since she was a teenager," Maria said regretfully. "We were angry that she didn't finish college as she was very smart. 'I kept up with my other children but I think that I pushed her away because I was afraid that Andrew would figure out the truth. 'I wasn't much of a mother to her...I will always regret that."

Just when he thought that he had no blood heirs this revelation happened, it was like a miracle. He wondered if she suffered much for being his child. It sounded like her mother had issues with her being around. Well he would make it up to her; a lifetime of love had to be packed into what few years he had left.

"I'm going to meet her," he said with joy in his heart.

First he felt that he had to know her, her habits and who she was—so he hired a detective to find out. It would be an exciting journey to study this special unexpected person in his life.

CHAPTER 24

Trying for an Interview

That afternoon Ed knocked on the door of room 110. He was anxious to get all this behind him so he could get some sleep. He was sure this was just a matter of a few quick questions before closing the case and going home. Tracy opened the door while in a pink *"Junior Rock Band"* inscribed T-shirt with the red sequent heart shape and what seemed like a pair of pink underwear, comfortable in thinking that it was one of the other's who had forgot their key. Shocked that it was the police officer from *Montgomery* and not knowing what to do, she simply slammed the door on Ed's face.

Ed stood there for a few seconds wondering what to do when the door re-opened again—but only a crack this time. Tracy peaked out slightly embarrassed at her own sudden reaction. After all she was an adult, she thought, even if she was in a child's T-shirt.

"Um, I'm sorry…I keep apologizing to you…what are you doing here…I mean can I help you?" she said in frustration.

He leaned toward her with one hand on the door frame and said with a cocky grin, "I followed you here from *Montgomery*… for AN official reason… can I come in and talk?"

"By the way, I like your shirt," he grinned sheepishly. He'd seen this brand on many teenagers.

"Is this related to your pulling us over the other night, are you going to arrest us…what did we do?" she sounded desperate and a little embarrassed of her attire.

"Relax you're not in trouble!! Is Nelly McMillan here?" he sounded formal again. "I need to talk to her."

As she relaxed and let Ed inside the door he mouthed the word "wow" behind Tracy's back as she turned to lead him into the room. He couldn't help but noticed beautiful long legs falling out below her pink t-shirt.

"Come sit on the patio with me, I've been trying to get some sun on my legs," she said casually as she breezed through the room. "Oh, and there is some sodas in the little frig over there."

She breezed through a disarrayed room and out of the patio door to sit in a lounge chair surrounded by barbed greenery, palm trees and sugary sand. Today the patio faced a peaceful part of the beach with very few sun bathers. Tracy was looking forward to the time alone but somehow wasn't too disappointed at Ed's sudden appearance.

"This is not a casual visit," he called as he suddenly felt unprofessional at joining her out on the patio but she ignored him.

Oh well, he thought as he shrugged his shoulders, went to the refrigerator to take up her offer for a cold drink and then walked out to the patio to pull up a plastic chair beside her. Feeling the heat through his cotton shirt, he loosened his tie and sipped from the coke can. While enjoying the cold liquid fizzing down his throat he felt guilty as he knew he needed to get to business—but the peacefulness of the moment seemed natural and preferable. He thought I'm sitting at the beach with a beautiful half naked woman; how much better can this get. His eyes followed Tracy's smooth legs from top to bottom with appreciation. As if on cue she picked up the suntan lotion and started to rub lotion into their smoothness. He swallowed hard and decided he needed a distraction so he'd get right down to business.

"I have a few questions for Nelly, where is she right now?" he asked hoarsely, then cleared his throat.

Tracy pointed toward the direction of a couple of Para-sailors over the ocean. From this distance they looked like ant sized bodies hanging loosely from tiny kites high above the white capped ocean. They seemed to be catching the winds, like seagulls hovering near the ocean shoreline. It was a natural part of the landscape…sand, seagulls, sunbathers and Para-sailors. An inflated banana boat stuffed full of swimsuit clad screaming tourists pulled by a jet ski buzzed across the scene.

"She's Para-sailing with Steve, aren't you a little out of your jurisdiction?" Tracy said lazily squinting out of one eye against the bright sun.

Ed didn't answer her but stared out at the ocean instead.

"I guess I should have gone but I just felt like lying around today," Tracy confessed guiltily as she reached for a pair of sun glasses.

Over to one side of the hotel, on a wooden deck, overlooking the beach, Ed noticed a small outdoor bar surrounded with palm trees. Why not buy a beer, he thought to himself. It was going to be sometime before Nelly came down from there and he was thirsty. Besides he needed the distraction.

"Get dressed," he commanded Tracy with a sudden smile, "I'll buy you a drink and we can talk." The coziness of the room was too much for him and he needed a public forum.

"I really don't want a drink right now, I'm just fine?" she told him sternly.

"Lady, at least get some clothes on," he took a chance at letting her know what was on his mind.

She popped up suddenly embarrassed at the thought of provoking this kind of reaction from him, "Alright, alright, give me a minute."

"Do you always run around in your underwear in front of Police Detectives?" he laughed.

"Detective? 'Were you promoted or something? 'Last time I met you, you were driving a squad car."

"Things change," Ed said casually.

"Besides, this is not my underwear, it's my swim wear."

As she got up he blew out the breath he was holding while mentally trying to cool his thoughts. This was one hot lady he thought as her pink swimsuit panties peeked below her shirt showing the tightest little butt he'd ever seen. His general feeling was that he could be arrested for his thoughts. He lingered out on the beach while he waited for Tracy to dress, his shoes sinking in the loose sand.

Tracy looked radiant in her new sundress and beach sandals as they cross behind *The Kumar Beach Resort* to its only bar. Her Carmel colored well styled hair and large hazel eyes stood out in the afternoon sun.

As they reached the bar area decorated in the Hawaii grass covered hut theme, Ed pulled out a wicker stool for Tracy to sit down at a table near the rail so they could keep an eye on the Para-sailors. A bar tender who looked barely legal asked them what they would have. Without asking her what she wanted, he ordered himself a beer and ordered her a glass of cooled white zinfandel wine.

She raised an eyebrow at this and asked, "How did you know I don't drink beer."

"Years on the force my dear, helps you size people up," he volunteered, "It makes you very intuitive."

"I thought that intuitive was only a word you used when describing old women." She teased.

"Can I ask you some questions about Nelly," He changed the subject after the drinks arrived.

She eyed him suspiciously, "I think that you should wait for Nelly."

"How is her relationship with her husband?" his asked as he ignored her last statement.

"I don't know much about that because we are mostly just co-workers but I can give you my opinion based on the conversations I've overheard." She lied trying to look casually.

"OK," he looked intent for her to continue.

"Well... he's known her since she was fifteen, I'm not sure when they married but I do know that he insisted before she was able to finish college, they had two children one when she was nineteen and they've been unhappily married for about twenty-nine years. Oh, and they argue on the phone a lot, that is well known by everyone at "*Aviation World*," Tracy put it shortly.

"So they fight on the phone?

"Actually, it's quite uncomfortable to hear her on the phone with him because as all she seems to constantly say is that she will try to do better, repeatedly," Tracy thought how she always knew when Nelly was on the phone with her husband.

"Really," he said out loud as he thought that the signs were there for this to turn out badly. He had better contact this jurisdiction to have the situation watched before returning to *Montgomery*. Ed felt that once he was back in *Montgomery*, maybe he could convince her husband to calm down and go home.

"I don't know anything about him other that he doesn't live in Atlanta and she travels many weekends commuting from her job to visit him in Memphis," she offered helpfully.

"Ok, well I tell you what, why don't we put this subject aside and enjoy the afternoon while I wait. I know of a little restaurant near the shore that makes the best crepes' any time of the day or night. Pancakes and crepes' make a good mid-afternoon snack, don't you think," he suggested looking hopeful for the right answer.

"Eeeek, I don't know, I've never eaten pancakes as a midday snack but I'll try it," Tracy said as she wrinkled up her nose. "Besides, I haven't eaten all day," she added.

Before leaving, Ed took one last look at the Para-sailors flying against blue sky and the sound of the call of seagulls; then he enjoyed one more breath of sea air before escorting Tracy to the Dodge Challenger. He might as well give up keeping an eye on the Para-sailors, he was convinced that they wouldn't come down for an hour or two and then he would have time to interview Nelly.

CHAPTER 25

Abby Meets Granny

Abby was bored!! She didn't really care that much for the beach and the others had their own way of enjoying themselves, which didn't really include her. First Nelly and Steve were on some adventure or another, right now Para Sailing, and then Tracy just wanted to sit on the patio doing nothing; all vacationing in their own style. Abby wanted to sit at a bar somewhere watching football games and drinking beer but she didn't know where to go. Nelly left her the keys to the PT Cruiser but it wasn't a good idea without a designated driver.

Abby plopped down on one of the lobby's sofas to think of where to go before noticing that she was next to Lillian's little Granny. The elderly woman was dressed in a sarong with a black braid hanging down to her waist. Although she was dressed in full Indian garb, her still smooth face looked troubled.

Abby couldn't remember being told Granny's name so she just called her what Lillian called her, "Hey Daa-dee-maa, remember me?"

Granny looked at Abby with intelligent eyes and snapped impatiently in a heavy accent, "Oh, of course I do you idiot, you're Lillian's acquaintance from *Montgomery*—I'm not senile."

Now Granny could just about get away with insulting people, but Abby was a different story. Abby would give the shirt off of her back but she also would never take abuse from anyone, no matter who that person.

"Wonderful Granny, I never said that you were senile…do you have something up you crawl?" Abby snapped back without regard to her elder. Abby thought, oh great, not only was she bored but now she was fighting with a ninety year old woman; however, Abby wasn't about to hold her tongue at anyone who snapped at her for no reason.

"What the hell is a crawl?" the tiny old women demanded again in a heavy accent with a twinkle in her eyes. She already liked this young women, she could tell that she didn't put up with anyone's shit.

"It's a …I don't now… It mean's what the fuck is bothering you?" Abby turned bright red at her own temper.

"I'll tell you what the fuck is bothering me" Granny reiterated, "Lillian is supposed to take me to mass and she doesn't have time. Now I have to listen to your foul mouth."

"You're Catholic!!" Abby said so loud that it drew attention.

"What's wrong with that, what did you think that I was?" Granny rolled her eyes.

"I don't know—Hindu or something like that," Abby had to say something to end this verbal battle.

"*You people* always stereo type, I was converted," Granny complained.

"No, it's just that I'm Catholic too and what's up with this *you people* anyway?" Abby explained, "Lillian always calls us *you people* too; like we are a bunch of aliens."

"White people ... are you stupid? You Catholic too ...then you take me to mass, I need to pray and go to confession," Granny demanded like it was her right.

"Oh no you don't, I'm not taking you or anyone else to mass, especially the way you talked to me," was Abby's first reaction.

Granny fell back against the sofa all huffed up and then she said meekly, "I'll be nicer if you take me to mass."

"Say Please," said Abby.

"Please," Granny responded

"Say Pretty Please," Abby teased.

Granny fell back again in a huff saying nothing for a full minute while Abby waited.

"OK, pretty please," Granny finally said humbly cutting her eyes at Abby.

"OK, lady, I'll go to mass with you but no more bad language and you have to behave yourself," Abby negotiated with a smile on her face, enjoying having the upper hand.

Granny slapped Abby hard on the knee, "I like you...you feisty like me."

"How come you not married," Granny looked at Abby's empty ring finger.

"I'm a widow, I had no choice, besides it's none of your damn business," Abby smiled indicating that she was enjoying the feisty old lady's verbal sparring too.

"You have a comfortable car or should I get my son's driver to take us?" Granny asked.

Abby responded by taking the Cruiser's keys out of her front pocket and dangling them in front of Granny.

"You go get your pocket book with your license and I'll wait here," Granny ordered as she readied herself for the wait.

Abby pulled her wallet out of her back pocket and showed Granny her license.

Granny's eyes went huge at the idea of Abby carrying a wallet like a man and asked directly, "are you gay?"

"Now I told you to be nice, I'm not gay and I don't answer to you, you old coot," Abby was really offended this time.

"Good, we shall go now," Granny smiled innocently.

As they shuffled to the door at Granny's speed Abby's voice trailed off, "are you always this mean...."

"Only to ignorant sluts ...but you are lovely young white woman...." Granny sidestepped diplomatically and grinned while looking up into Abby's face.

The cathedral was an unexpected historical pleasure. Instead of a large modern brick building with a wealth of stain glass windows, it turned out to be a small old white wooden church with a bell tower dating back to the mid1800s. The congregation sat surrounded by an oak carved but creaky old balcony circling the sanctuary. In the front was a single stain glass window in the shape of a cross. The pulpit sat raised in the center just before the cross. It had the faint smell of a musty old building.

A CHANGE OF LUCK

Abby thought that the one thing she always admired about the Catholic Church was that no matter what cathedral she went to, it was always felt like she was home. There was a since of familiarity in Catholicism that no protestant church could provide or understand.

After a very satisfying service was over, Granny seemed peaceful and gently stated, "I will repay you by cooking your dinner tonight. You will like Indian food."

As Abby drove down the sand salted road bleached by the sun, she casually told Granny that Nelly had told them that they were invited to dinner with her son at the hotel tonight.

Granny's demeanor changed as she sat up and demanded, "No, you will come eat with me and so will the rest of them. 'He did not ask my permission to arrange such a dinner with guests."

She continued, "We have honor guests at the mansion, not at the hotel like a business meeting!"

"Calm down, Granny, it will all be good. Why don't you come with me," which was the wrong thing to say.

In the passenger seat of the car Granny suddenly clutched her heart and tried to catch her breath.

"You take me to the emergency room, I am having a heart attack," she demanded.

Abby felt panic well up in her throat as she had no experience with heart attacks, what should she do. "I'll call 911 and have an ambulance meet us but I am not driving you to the emergency room in your condition," she said desperately.

"Get a hold of yourself you stupid woman, it's just a couple of blocks away," Granny yelled still clutching her chest.

"Oh no, you didn't just call me stupid after I took you to church!!!" now Abby didn't care if Granny was having a heart attack or not, she was not going to put up with this old fool. Abby pulled the car over to the side of the road and demanded an apology before she drove on.

"Ok, call the ambulance if you want, but you will have to ride two blocks in an ambulance with me and leave your car here," Granny said while still clutching her chest in the act of pain.

Abby saw the reasoning and restarted her car.

"Alright, you win but only because you're having a heart attack," Abby said as she desperately drove on wondering why this elderly women affected her this way. She should never have pulled over to the side of the road when someone, anyone, was having a heart attack, no matter what their attitude. Time was critical.

Granny led them to a circular drive marked by a huge sign that said *Kumar Medical Center Emergency Room*. Abby jumped out and grabbed the first nurse she could find. The nurse immediately recognized Granny, grabbed a wheelchair and put her on it, then pushed her into room number two. The nurse connected her up to the heart monitor, and checked her oxygen levels before ordering another nurse to call her doctor, and then her son.

Abby called Tracy and instructed her to find Lillian.

As Abby came back, Granny lay pitiful looking on a gurney. She heard the nurse call Granny Mrs. Kumar and realized that the Emergency ward had the name Kumar before it. Abby wanted to ask about her relationship to the name but a flurry of EKG techs and lab techs rushed in and out of the room, interrupting them. Then a distinguished looking Indian gentleman entered though the dividing curtain. His eyes were large and had the same mischievous sparkle as Granny.

"What are you doing up here again?" Christopher Kumar demanded of his mom.

"She's having a heart attack you idiot," Abby was now protective of Granny, "who the hell are you to talk to her like that?"

"I'm her son! This is my mother—so who the … are you!!" he yelled back as he stopped short of cussing.

Granny took a deep breath from her nasal canella and moaned weakly, "this is my friend, Abby, who has been gracious enough to bring me to the emergency room so be respectful of my guest and Abby please don't cuss."

"Why the hell not, you do," Abby accused.

"Mine sounds so much better because I have a Hindu accent," Granny replied.

"Bullshit," Abby shot back.

At this Christopher smirked as he thought the old lady had finally met her match.

"Why did you plan a dinner without telling me…I might as well die if my children forget about me," again Granny moan weakly.

Abby finally got it. All this was about the dinner. Granny was acting out a heart attack over a damn dinner.

"I get it, Granny did you fake a heart attack to spoil your son's damn dinner plans?" Abby asked bluntly.

Granny sat up and pulled the oxygen out of her nose and pointed at her son, "I am in charge of this family...he was sneaking behind my back to have a damn dinner without my permission."

Then Granny pointed at Abby, "Abby gave me such a lovely afternoon, I have decided that you and Abby shall get married within the week. I have spoken."

Abby watched in shock while Granny laid back down on the gurney and put on her oxygen; her long black braid tangling up with the tube.

"You crazy, insane old woman...what world did you come from...you can't just order people to get married," Abby said in frustration.

At this point Christopher Kumar was enjoying Abby's discomfort and thought it amusing to increase Abby's discomfort by calling what he thought was his mom's bluff.

"If you're sure mom, I will get Lillian to start the wedding plans. 'We'll have to give everyone enough time to fly in from India," Christopher wanted to burst out laughing at Abby's expression but contained himself. It was actually refreshing to see this little slip of a white woman stand up to his formidable mother

Abby looked from mother to son, "This is a joke right?"

"Oh, no joke, Mom here is a very powerful woman with vast holdings. She owns the hotels you've been staying in and even donated this emergency ward." Christopher mocked. "We are like the Indian mafia and I run her holdings so I have to do as she asks, just like in the old country. If mom says there is to be a wedding, there is to be a wedding."

Just then Lillian entered through the same curtain patrician where her uncle entered, "wedding, what wedding?"

"Mother has ordered that Abby and I get married right away and you are to make the arrangements," Christopher said barely containing himself at this stranger's reaction of losing her tongue. Did she really think that he was serious?

Lillian was relieved that it wasn't her wedding but felt sorry for Abby, "Hello Abby, *you people* are joking aren't you?"

"Of course not my child, I will want to see you get started in the morning…no get started tonight…I want the entire family, the prince of Kawate and everyone is to be notified," Granny talked dreamily as she lay on the starchy white sheets.

Abby found her tongue, "This is not going to happen, Lillian, so don't listen to these fools."

Christopher ignored Abby and iterated, "Lillian, you know Abby too?"

"Of course, her and her friends drove me here from *Montgomery*; she's been staying at the hotel," Lillian explained while putting down her purse and reaching over Granny to offer her a drink of water.

Granny didn't get this far in life playing the fool and said softly, "Christopher you will be disinherited if you do not follow through with my orders."

"Ok, wait a minute, Granny you know this is not going to happen no matter how much you threaten, manipulate or fake heart attacks. I was your friend but I will not be your friend if you keep this up," Abby had her attention now. "All you'll be remembered for is a spoiled old woman."

"No Abby, I'm a grateful old woman who is giving you her greatest prize, my son, for being kind enough to put up with an old woman for one remarkable afternoon. In our culture it is my right as matriarch of the family and the family will honor this one request. From here on out I will make no more arranged marriages...and I will release all my holdings to my sons—that's if you honor this request. I am getting tired and I need someone of your wit, strength and wisdom to take my place," she said as she rolled over to face the wall.

Christopher lowered his head so Abby couldn't see what he was thinking and Lillian looked at Abby hopefully. So basically, Abby thought, this crazy old woman was saying I'll get off of my families back if, I, Abby, marry her son, a complete stranger—and Granny apparently has the clout and money it takes to make it happen.

"Your friends are out in the lobby," Lillian said softly.

Abby left soberly and quietly.

"Daa-dee-maa, please you can't do this to Abby, be reasonable," Lillian pleaded.

Christopher liked Abby, she certainly was feisty, which was refreshing to him, but he couldn't see her as his wife. She looked too much like a boy; right down to the baseball cap. Her hair was short, she wore clothes like a man and she cussed...like...well...his little sweet Indian mother. He didn't really care if he lost the holdings, he had put enough away to start on his own but his brothers would be devastated. Yes this marriage would have to take place, even if it was just all staged. He would make it worth Abby's while and Abby could carry on as she pleased after the wedding. He would buy her off. Everyone has a price.

As Abby entered the hospital waiting room, simply decorated with green armless leather seated chairs, her first words to her friends were, "we have got to get out of town as soon as possible."

A CHANGE OF LUCK

They didn't really know what to say to this and were speechless.

When Abby looked around she noticed two more members added to the small group. "Wait a minute she said, "The police officer I recognizable but who is the Native American? Where is Nelly?"

Steve explained that He and Nelly had come with Lillian and that Tracy had just arrived. He told Abby that Nelly said that she would be right back as she needed some water to take some aspirin for being sore from Para-sailing. Finally he said as he ran out of breath, "I don't know the 'native American' he came with Lillian."

Lillian answered as she entered, "I've invited him to dinner…his name is Nick… he saved a woman from a shark in the water behind our hotel."

Before Abby could comment Christopher Kumar had followed Lillian out to the waiting room and demanded that he be introduced to Abby's friends. Then changed his mind and decided to call for a limousine driver to take the small crowd back to the hotel. He told everyone that all this could be sorted out over dinner.

In hopes of finding time to question Nelly, Ed decided to step in and organize everyone, "We have our cars and we don't need a driver but I'm certain that everyone is hungry so if everyone is agreeable we will take you up on the dinner. We'll meet you back at the hotel."

Steve didn't want to be organized; he wanted answers now, "So let me understand, basically, we have the detective from *Montgomery* here, the guy who saved a lady from a Shark and the four of us? Let's first start out with the important question. Lillian, is your Granny OK?"

"Daa-dee-maa is fine, I'll arrange a sitter for the night and then meet you people at the hotel for dinner," Lillian said as she eyed Abby who had collapsed in a chair near the courtesy phone. Abby had encountered hurricane Granny and Lillian could see that it was taking its toll. She could identify with Abby's feelings.

"OK, having gotten that out of the way, what is with Abby?" Steve demanded. He had grown fond of these women, they were his friends and he felt obligated to protect them.

"Hurricane Granny… but I'll explain it to you people at the hotel," Lillian waved a hand to indicate for Christopher to wait as he started to open his mouth. "I will meet you all at the hotel. Uncle, as you so wisely suggested, we can sort all this out over dinner.

Ed looked around for Nelly, Where the hell was Nelly throughout all this? He was having a heck of a time catching up with this woman. If he didn't get this straightened out soon, he'd catch it from the chief and possible be fired. This was just supposed to be a quick interview, leave it to the new jurisdiction and then back home. Just then his cell phone rang.

"Hey Jack, what's up," Ed answered waiting for the inevitable questions relating to the case being wound up yet.

"The lady's husband checked out and we don't know where he has gone. 'Ed, we missed the gun in the hotel safe and he has it with him," Jack said worriedly, "If this all escalates and we do nothing about it, I see a potential law suit. 'I've gotten in touch with the FBI and they requested that you stay with the women until they get there. 'Carrying a gun across state lines without a license is a federal offence, plus we think that he filed a false police report to use police resources to find her."

He hung up, thinking that Jack's timing was impeccable. He was stuck for the night anyway, or at least until he could catch up with Nelly.

Tracy looked at him with a question in her lovely hazel eyes and he secretly hoped that she wouldn't get in the middle of all this. He didn't want her to get hurt. He couldn't explain why he felt this way.

"Tracy, where's Nelly?" he asked.

"I don't know," Tracy said as she looked around the room.

"She should be back by now, what's going on, what do you want with Nelly?" Steve felt Ed's nervousness.

Ed paused a second to think on the repercussions of letting her friends in on police business. It wasn't his precinct's policy to disclose suspicions or recruit help to find a victim. However, he personally needed help to search the hospital and time may be critical; she had been gone longer than expected and that was suspicious. If he unnecessarily called in the troops and she was just meandering around the hospital halls unharmed…well it was a hard judgment.

"We need to find her and I'll tell you why later. 'Just the fact that I'm here may tell you something," was all Ed said.

"I don't believe that we have met but I will assist by utilizing hospital security," Christopher said with a since of generality toward the proper procedure. He was a member of the hospital board and well recognized by the staff, this would help.

"Would the Lady's please remain here and the Gentlemen please follow me," Christopher requested.

He may as well been talking to the wall as the women were way ahead of his request.

CHAPTER 26

We Finally Catch Up

Nelly opened a single packet of aspirin that she had bought at the gift shop and threw it to the back of her throat before swigging from the water fountain to wash it down. She was so sore from her adventures the last couple of days that she could hardly move. She was in pretty good shape from jogging but this was different. As she stood up she wiped the remaining drips of water from her mouth with the back of her hand and looked around. Night was approaching and it seemed that most of the visitors had gone home; the empty hall seemed to echo only one last visitor. There was a character leaning against the wall in the shadows, opposite the direction of the Gift shop. He looked familiar.

As David stepped out into the light she immediately recognized him. Suddenly chills ran down her spine as his eyes had a crazy glaze in them.

"Remember me, your husband," he asked nonchalantly.

"David…how…what are you doing here?" she was at a loss for words.

"Never mind, love, I came to bring you home," he sounded threatening. His eyes looked like the life had gone out of them and something evil replaced it.

"Don't be ridicules David, I can't. ' I'm driving and my friends are depending on me," she tried to sound nonchalance but her voice shook. Something was wrong with David. He looked like a mountain lion about to pounce on a bunny rabbit.

"David, what's wrong with you; you look… weird," she decided to directly get to the heart of the matter.

She remembered when she first saw David. He was a man and she was a teenager of fifteen but somehow she knew that he was the one she would marry. With his dark good looks and long graceful muscular legs, he was the most fascinating man in the world to her. He had a broad smile and corny since of humor; and he was gorgeous. She fell for him right away but, like a true gentleman, he wouldn't date her until she was older. When she finally turned eighteen, they married right away. She was eighteen and he was twenty-eight when they had their first child. She should have left him after their first child but instead she spent a lifetime hoping to find something of the man she loved when she was a teenager.

"You're going home, Nelly …that's final. I won't have my wife running all over the countryside with strange men, you remember what happened last time," he hissed under his breath. Their relationship was compared to a quiet peaceful mountain that was actually an undetected volcano; first there was the natural splendor of the mountain, then there was the sudden unexpected explosion that blackened the atmosphere and then the toxic grey ash that chocked out the living beauty—it took years for the mountain grow back to its original splendor. It seemed like their love was chocked out by toxic grey ash and that she was just patiently waiting for things to return to their original splendor; however, now she realized that the ash was just too toxic. She felt that it was her fault as she had ruined everything but now she knew she had to let go.

Nelly had to say the words she feared saying for years, her throat tightened and with tears rolling down her cheeks, she whispered, "David, you and I are over."

David reached into the back of his belt and pulled out the little automatic browning pistol. While waving it at her he yelled, "You are never to say that to me again, do you hear me…NEVER!"

"Please David don't do this to yourself, what about the children," Nelly pleaded as she was truly scared what would happen to David.

He repeated her words mockingly then said, "You are the one that is doing this to them by trying to break up our little fam-i-ly; but I won't let that happen."

As luck would have it, Ed happened up on the last part of David's conversation and realized that his partner Jack's fear of this not ending well was about to be realized. He wished that he had put on his bullet proof vest. He had drawn his gun very few times in his career as a police officer; but he knew what to do.

The rest of the group all converged down on each other from different directions to haphazardly meet in hall in front of the gift shop and just behind Ed. Ed put his hand up to signal for the group to come to a halt and pointed a finger to go back to safety.

Nick herded everyone back behind his body shielding the three women.

"David I'm the police officer from *Montgomery*, put the weapon down and place your hands on the wall before someone gets hurt," Ed tried to coax David.

David a shot the browning past Nelly at Ed but the bullet missed. Instead it shattered the glass window of the gift shop, spewing shards of sharp glass all over the vestibule—it was like a crystal explosion. A shopper screamed at the sudden sound of the bullet whizzing by her cheek to end its journey lodged in the stuffed panda bear that she was holding. Being the ones closest to the window, Nick had quickly grabbed Lillian and pressed her against his chest, turning his back to shield her from the flying glass shards. One of the shards ripped through his back making a four inch gash and Lillian immediately begin to tend to the injury by trying to stop the blood.

Ed dodged to one side and tried to take aim but by this time David had Nelly by her hair and held the gun to her head. Without a word he backed back down the hall to a side exit where he had parked his car.

"I will kill her if you follow," David called to Ed as he exited the building.

Before following them, Ed instructed Christopher to call the police. Then he ran out the door with Steve bravely in tow.

The police detective and the coworker of Nelly happened to run out the side entrance just in time to see the little green Honda speeding out of its parking space through the half empty parking lot toward the attendant's booth. There didn't seem to be any hope of catching up with them so Ed holstered his gun and stood in fear of knowing what could happen to Nelly; however, Steve kept running without regard to his own safety; maybe out nothing else to do.

Just then a Toyota Tundra backed out of a parking space ramming into the side of the Honda which slowed the Honda down. Nelly saw her opportunity and jumped out the passenger side, rolling out into the parking lot. She figured if she could escape a hungry alligator, she could escape a mad husband. She had to do it to protect both of them. If David killed her, their children would have a murderer for a father; but if he had some time to think about his actions he may come to his senses, serve a little time and it would be over.

With Nelly no longer in the car, he stopped to consider his options before driving on to smash through the toll booth and down the road. The attendant of the toll booth saw him coming and managed to get out of the way just in time before the wooden booth splintered and was tossed over the top of the Honda.

Nelly lay on the black tar pavement staring at the dusky sky. The fall had knocked the wind out of her lungs and she struggled hard to suck the air back into them. Finally, as she tried to breathed, she sat up to see concern in the eyes of the driver of the Toyota Tundra. He was a short man with dark curly hair.

"Lady are you OK?" he looked like he wouldn't have known what to do if she wasn't.

As she was gasped successfully for her breath, Steve arrived.

"I think that I'm OK, but my ribs hurt," Nelly answered a little dazed.

Having caught up with Nelly, Steve really didn't know what to do. He was too much man to cry at her being OK but scared to touch her in case something was broken. He stood there looking helpless.

Feeling Steve's helplessness, Nelly decided to make him smile so she reached past the pain to make a joke, "MAN, WHAT A RUSH!"

"Dam it Nelly, how can you make a joke out of this... you could have been killed," he was angry but the driver from the truck snickered.

"She is one tough lady as a couple days ago she escaped another type of attack…I don't know why she is still alive," Steve told the driver of the small truck.

With Nelly still sitting on the pavement, Steve put his hand out hand to the driver of the truck and introduced himself, "I'm Steve, and I want to thank you for saving her life, she was kidnapped by an idiot. Are you OK?"

"My pleasure, my name is Mike," Mike Coffer said as he purposely left off his last name. Nick was going to have to hire someone else to follow Nelly. She would recognize him if he tried to follow her now. However their client would be happy to know that Mike had earned his money by protecting Mr. Durrell's concern and also that it was company policy to buy insurance on the rental vehicles, because this one was probably totaled.

"Can you help me up?" Nelly pointed out that she was still sitting on the pavement.

"Sure, but is that wise, shouldn't we call a doctor or something," Mike wondered as he held a hand out to Nelly.

As she stood she felt sore but guessed that nothing was broken. She brushed the dirt from the back of her pants and walked in a circle to relieve the stiffness—the stiffness was there to begin with; therefore, she wasn't sure if her soreness was from jumping out of a car, Para-sailing or being thrown by an alligator. She just knew that her life was turned upside down and the soreness keep her mind off the emotional mess she made.

"I'm sorry about your truck," Nelly apologized to Mike.

"It's OK, I have insurance," Mike looked it over as Ed finally arrived.

It seemed lucky that the proximity of the Emergency room was nearby as both Nelly and Nick were seen by busy doctors in record time. Nelly had bruised her ribs and Nick needed four stitches to close a laceration on his back; however, much to Ed's relief, everyone survived the ordeal.

Before everyone left for the hotel, the local police came and took a detailed report. Ed received a copy for his department and he thanked them for their time.

At the hotel Nelly made her apologies for not attending dinner and went straight to their room to sleep off the pain medicine that the doctor prescribed. She was aching all over and hoped that she would feel better in the morning. Regardless of everything that had happened, she still had every intention of continuing on to *Biloxi* where John would take care of their room, she had to get away. She hadn't told the others yet but she would convince them in the morning. Right now all she wanted to do was to soak in a hot tub of water and sleep.

CHAPTER 27

A Late Dinner

    The hotel's private dining room was richly decorated in the same sandy colored scheme as the rooms. The difference in the wall paper was that narrow sliver streamers were tastefully embedded along pictures of translucent seashells. The long glass dining table had a large well lit tropical fish aquarium full of coral as its base so one could see multicolored angel fish swimming beneath the gold flicked silverware settings. Linen napkins with the emblem Kumar sewed into the corner were held together with ivory colored china napkin rings. On a buffet table against one wall sat a modest row of banquet trays with candles flickering beneath to keep the food warm. Soft classical music came out of invisible speakers. Two servers smartly dressed in matching white shirts and khaki shorts stood at either end of the buffet table awaiting orders.

    Tracy felt intimidated at the elegance and tried to smooth the wrinkles from her dress before iterating, "This is a beautiful room."

"Well it's late and let's not stand on formality, please everyone help yourself to the buffet table," Christopher offered.

Steve's belly had overridden his since of intimidation toward the stylish décor so, without shyness, he rushed to buffet table which helped to break the proverbial ice; and the usual sense of politeness toward who should go first. Then Nick encouraged Lillian to go before him; then Ed, Tracy, Abby and the host went last. The meal consisted of prairie dusted steaks, broiled chicken covered with spicy peanut sauce, tilapia with mango sauce, asparagus spears, squash flavored cornbread dressing and rice pilaf. They were offered mint tea laced with a small amount of liquor.

As they were eating Christopher was curious concerning Nelly's adventures and Steve told the story of the tour into the swamp. They all laughed at the coastguard having to drag them and the jet skis back across the bay. Then they all expressed concern for Nelly's misadventure at the hospital.

"I will ensure her safety here at the hotel until all this is worked out…I have a security guard that can watch her door and we have security camera's in each hall, as well as the lobby," he said with a gentlemanly obligation toward his responsibility as the manager of the hotel and responsibility for protecting his guests.

"The security guard won't be necessary, I will follow through with the FBI in the morning and see that she is safe throughout the night," Ed suddenly didn't like the idea of a civilian becoming involved.

Lillian felt the tension and decided to change the subject. As she raised her glass she announced, "We are here to say thanks to our friends. 'To the ladies who saw me safely to my Uncle, to Abby for making my Grandmother happy for an afternoon and also to the Shark Fighter, I say thanks." Everyone raised their crystal glasses and toasted.

Nick set his glass down and was truly touched by Lillian's description of himself as the Shark Fighter. His mother would like that name. Then, while scooting a piece of steak across his half empty plate, he decided to let the others in on the real reason for his being here in *Panama City Beach*."

It probably didn't matter now, he thought as he started to confess, "I don't usually betray trusts but I am somewhat invested in all this." They all looked at Nick as if he was an alien and a free radical. His only reason for being a part of the group was by Lillian's invitation, how could he be invested?

Lillian's eyes softened as she had become sensitive to the nature of this man who became a hero in her eyes. Twice in one day he came to the rescue. However, just as he was about to explain himself, his Nextel cell phone rang and he excused himself to go out in the hall. Lillian's disappointment showed…what did he mean by "invested"…was Nick in love with Nelly? Nelly was an older women but very attractive and a lot of younger men were involved with older women these days.

Were they having an affair? Is that why David was so jealous?

"Yeah, Mike, what is it?" Nick's question echoed down the empty hall.

"Look Nick, I know that you want me to take over for you but…well…to put it bluntly, I was the driver of the Toyota truck today. I saw that bastard come out the side entrance with a gun to her head and I figured that it would be the right thing to do to block his way out of the parking lot. I didn't succeed, but I did slow him down long enough for her to jump out. Also, I wrecked the truck…sorry about that," he reported.

"You did good Mike," Nick consoled him, "I believe that our client would agree. 'Listen, get another rental car and stay on it as long as you can, at least until I get some rest."

"One other thing, Mr. Durrell is flying to *Panama City Beach* tomorrow to meet with us tomorrow," Mike reported.

"Damn, this is not a good time, well, like I said, stay on it through the night and let's see what happens in the morning. 'Maybe we'll be finished with the case in a day or two; then we both can go home," Nick hung up the phone without saying goodbye.

After Nick had reentered the dining room, everyone but Lillian had forgotten that Nick was about to divulge his "investment" in all this. Changing his mind about coming clean, he decided to make his excuses by saying, "Well, I'm tired, I'll check on Nelly's room before I go to bed."

Lillian didn't know why his leaving the room to check on Nelly depressed her so badly. She thought that she just barely met the man. She wondered if she could be jealous of Nelly, "the little green monster can rear its ugly head at any time," her mother once said. She couldn't look at Nick in fear of him reading her mind so instead she studied an Angle fish as it swam through a small piece of coral under her plate. Suddenly she knew how David felt as she really would like to tear Nelly's hair out right now. No, she would never be like David; if Nick and Nelly were in love, she only wanted the best for them. Then she thought, this is crazy, they don't even know each other.

Ed started to protest at Nick checking on Nelly but then decided that it didn't hurt to have others check on Nelly. After all, these were her friends and they wanted to feel like they were doing something for her.

Steve offered for Ed to stay in his room and asked Abby to bunk with Tracy. Christopher gave Abby a surprised look, "Your staying with Steve?"

"Not really," she didn't know why she needed to explain, "There is an extra bed in Steve's room where I sleep so we can all have our own bed, nothing physical."

"Then I shall provide another room for the men," he announced.

"That won't be necessary, my bed is plenty big to share," Tracy offered.

Ed asked Tracy to have another drink at the bar with him before they went to bed and Steve made his excuses leaving Abby alone with Christopher.

"Before you retire, I'd like to talk to you about what mother said today," He requested formally, "but first walk with me on the beach while we digest."

"Well, OK but there is nothing to talk about," Abby reminded him.

They stopped by the hotel desk to remind the clerk to set up a security guard in the hall of room 110 and then they pressed on through the glass doors leading to the beach.

"Abby I know that this is all ludicrous to you but to my mother its real, arranged marriages have been a part of our family tradition for generations. 'Grant it that this is America and we need to comply with American traditions, but there are still some things that can't be changed," he went on with what seemed like an apology for his mother.

"Your mother is one of them," she giggled at the thought of the feisty older women.

He smiled at her little joke and stopped just short of the surf before causing his expensive shoes to become wet, "Well yes, let me talk Abby. 'Abby, I'll get to the point.' If you will marry me like my mother requests, I will buy you anything you request as a wedding present and you have no *physical* obligation."

She looked into his dark eyes to ensure that this wasn't a joke, that he was actually serious.

"Christopher I may not be attracted to you, or are you me and I won't be in a sexless marriage. 'You seem like the type that likes prissy little women in lace with gold painted china tea cups and I have no intention of becoming something I'm not.' You know that this just won't work," she tried to reason with him.

While he looked over her head at the ocean she studied his face. He was an attractive man whom she could find pleasure in getting to know but she also knew right away that there were too many differences. She like to eat off of a TV tray while watching Nascar; he ate in an elegant dining hall over a well kept fish tank, meanwhile listening to classical music. She looked forward to The Monster Truck Rally once a year while he looked forward to whatever he does, but she knew one thing for sure, it wasn't The Monster Truck Rally. She carried her dead husband's ashes in her truck for heaven's sake.

"Nelly, it's just a business arrangement. 'You can go on with your life however you want and I won't interfere, plus you will have all my assets at your discretion.' As they say, all of the perks none of the responsibility," he promised.

"Anything?"

"Yes," he said as he looked into her eyes, "anything…well within reason."

"We're both widows married once to the love of our lives so what can it hurt to have a business arrangement. 'Here is the deal, I don't have to wear a dress to wedding and you will buy me *Aviation World*… and a Monster Truck.' Also, I'll need an allowance of $5000.00 a month."

He laughed, "If that is all you want, it's a deal." His mother was right about Abby, she would go far as most women would ask for expensive jewelry or another mansion. A business was actually a good investment to add to the family portfolio. Five thousand a month was actually chump change for the wife of a Multimillionaire.

"That's all I want, I'm not greedy," she smiled at his humor.

"Just how did you come by all this money?"

"I didn't, my mom did," he explained, "but it belongs to me and my brothers when she passes on."

"How did she get all this money?"

"Mom was sixteen when my father fell in love with her. 'He was thirty years older than her and had two other wives. 'He was also a diplomat. 'The marriage was arranged. 'In India when women become married, they aren't giving pots and pans as in America, they are given jewelry. 'With her husband being a diplomat, she was actually given nearly a treasure chest of very expensive gold jewelry, diamonds and emeralds; probably not that expensive in India, but in America… 'My father died just after my youngest brother was born so our mother left us with our Grandparents and came to the United States to start a new life. 'She used some of her jewelry as a down payment on one hotel and soon she owned a chain of hotels. 'She then used those profits to create an investment company and the rest is history," he told his mother's story.

Abby was suddenly impressed with the women that she bantered with this afternoon and said, "She was a brave and smart woman."

"As she was able, she sent for us children one at a time. 'She also sent money back home to my youngest brother so that he could remain in India and do mission work as a doctor. 'She has had to be tough all her life but she does a lot of good," he continued to speak well of his mother with love in his voice. Just then Abby realized that he didn't feel like he was obligated to follow his mother's order to marry, but he wanted to because he loved and respected her.

"You must have been pretty young when she sent for you because you barely have an accent," Abby noticed.

"Yes, I was the oldest, well technically I was an identical twin born second but my twin died at birth, so I had the pleasure of coming to the U.S.A. first," he agreed, "Unlike the others, she sent me to public schools and acclimatized me as much as possible. 'She had plans for me taking her position as the C.E.O. of the Kumar Company Holdings."

"About the physical part," Abby said boldly as she changed the subject, "someday I may need that to happen, that is if you don't find me too disgusting. 'I won't be able to go without sex all my life."

"Ok, I will arrange a honeymoon and see what happens… that is if you don't find me too disgusting," he laughed.

"Alright, it's a deal," she said and then reached out to shake his hand.

Instead he carefully pulled off her ball cap, fluffed up her short blond hair and with a caressing finger, gently teased her full lips; meanwhile whispering near her left ear, "I don't find you disgusting, Abby…not at all…Thank you…I know how hard this if for you." Then he handed her back her hat, turned and walked across the white sand back to the hotel.

As she stood there listening to the waves and looking at the stars, she thought that he definitely knew what to do with women. He could get more of a reaction from a woman's body with one finger than most men could with their entire body.

She threw her ball cap down in the waves and watched it grow heavy with water before sinking. She knew that she'd never wear it again. Then she walked over to the patio leading to their room and sat down on Tracy's lounge chair to look up at the clear summer sky full of bright stars and to breathe the fresh ocean air. She had to think but instead she soon fell asleep under the night sky.

CHAPTER 28

Sunday Morning

Nelly opened her eyes at the sound of soft knocking at the door. As she looked over in the next bed, she expected to see Tracy but instead saw Steve rolled up in a bunch of covers with bare limbs hanging out. Apparently he now felt comfortable enough with the women that he wore what he wanted and she started feeling comfortable with him too, almost like a brother.

"Steve, wake up, where's Tracy?" she asked as she still lay in one place, still too sore to move.

Just then Tracy stirred in the doorway leading into Steve's room. "I'm in Steve's room," she said as she smiled, taking a sip of coffee and disappeared back into Steve's room.

"Now do you understand," Steve said as he yawned, turned over, and tried to go back to sleep.

Before Nelly had time to think about what Steve said, Abby came in through the sliding glass doors rubbing her stiff back from sleeping in the lounge all night. "Is any one going to answer the door," she said as she stretched. Then she slowly walked over and answered the door.

"Where did you sleep last night?" Nelly asked but Abby was too intent on answering the door to answer Nelly.

Lillian came bursting into the room and with excitement hugged Abby while ranting something about a wedding, "Oh my Gosh, this is so exciting…I can't wait for the wedding. 'Christopher has me already making plans.' I'm supposed to come up with Hindu style wedding clothes—but no dress."

"Wedding!!" Nelly said out loud, "What is going on?"

"Granny has arranged a wedding between Christopher and Abby. 'I didn't think that Ms. Abby would agree—but Christopher said that Ms. Abby agreed last night. 'He wants to start the wedding plans immediately."

"Hindu, I'm Catholic!" Abby again seemed to ignore Nelly.

"You don't understand, it will be a Catholic wedding but we like to honor our culture with respect to our friends and family with Hindu wedding garments. 'Hopefully that won't be an issue with you," Lillian said excitedly, "I have sent a design to a seamstress in India to start sewing authentic red silk britches with gold brocade. 'Trust me your wedding will be perfect. 'The date will be next week all Saturday afternoon starting at Granny's church."

"You mean that you and Christopher are getting married?" Nelly seemed in shock.

"You bet, Granny arranged it," Abby didn't feel like going into detail.

"Granny?" Nelly was confused, "I thought that she had a heart attack."

A CHANGE OF LUCK

"Oh, that's right, you haven't met her yet," Abby remembered.

Just then Ed and Tracy came out of Steve's room in matching robes with *The Kumar Inn Beach Resort* embossed on them.

"Boy, let a husband kidnap you once and you miss out on all the excitement—You and Ed?" Nelly asked Tracy.

Tracy blushed and nodded.

Nelly knew that she had to think quickly as for some psychic reason she felt that this trip wasn't supposed to end at *Panama City Beach* but instead *Biloxi*. Right now it looked like the other ladies were set on staying. The incident at *Aviation World* was just days ago but it seemed like years ago, everything in their lives had changed.

"Ok… well… it's an American tradition for the friends of the Bride to have a Bachelorette party and I think that we ought to drive on to *Biloxi* for a day or two to celebrate Abby's wedding," Nelly suggested addressing Lillian as she prayed that they would buy into her scheme to get them to *Biloxi*. This was the ticket that would convince them to go.

"That's a great idea!" Tracy jumped in on the band wagon.

"Sure," said Abby a little indifferently.

Ed looked a little worried, "You are in danger Nelly, and you can't just go traipsing across the countryside unprotected."

"Nonsense, David has no idea that I'm going to *Biloxi* but he knows I'm here; it will be perfect."

"You've got a point," Ed said as he disappeared back into Steve's room. Tracy caught Nelly's eyes, smiled, raised her eyebrows and then followed Ed back through the door.

"That's great," Nelly said truly happy for Tracy as the two of them disappeared back into Steve's room.

"Yeah, at least someone around here is getting some action," Steve laughed

"Oh, you want some action, Steve," Abby teased, "I still haven't had my threesome yet."

"You are going to be married women soon," Steve acted insulted.

At that, Abby decided to take a shower and Lillian decided to follow Abby into the bathroom to talk through the shower curtain about the wedding, leaving Steve and Nelly alone.

"Nelly, it's time for me to go back home. 'I have to work tomorrow…I have a daughter to support. 'I'll see if the hotel has an airport shuttle?" he sounded almost apologetic.

"I understand," she said sad to see this happen as they had all become "comrades in arms."

"I'm sorry about your husband, but your one powerful women, you'll make it through this with Ed's help. 'David must be a dirt bag to do this to his wife," he felt guilty about leaving her in this mess. She was on suspension from work and her husband was trying to kidnap her.

"You don't understand," Nelly looked suddenly like the weight of the world was on her shoulders.

She hesitated and then took a deep breath before saying, "Steve it's my entire fault."

"How could your husband trying to kill you be your fault," he was surprised at Nelly's interpretation of David's behavior.

She looked ashamed and then confessed something that she had never confessed before spilling out her heart told her secret story, "Steve, I had an affair about ten years ago, David has never been the same since. 'He found an email where I wrote a love letter and he just went crazy. 'I thought I loved the guy, Marlow was his name. 'It was awful; I was obsessed with him and was just about to leave David for him when I found out that Marlow was married and also that he had other women. 'Anyway, David tried to kill himself and was in the hospital recovering for several weeks. 'I felt so bad that I kept taking baths to clean Marlow off of my skin. 'It's a wonder that I didn't catch a disease and give it to David. 'Anyway, David took me back but it hasn't been the same since."

Steve didn't know what to say, it was something that he didn't expect from the women he begun to see as his friend. Suddenly, with her confession, she just seemed like another slut that ruined a man's life.

Having been through a wife who cheated on him, he suddenly couldn't relate to Nelly. He didn't like Nelly for what she did to her husband and he both physically and mentally turned his back on her. It was like a mask of emotional unavailability creped through the room, almost like it was a living, breathing, entity. His disapproval tore at Nelly's heart.

"I'm sorry for letting you down," she attempted to apologize.

"I got to get going," he said coldly without acknowledgement.

Nelly started to cry at Steve's reaction; meanwhile Tracy heard the last part of the conversation from the door and stared at Steve.

Feeling uncomfortable under Tracy's stare, Steve yelled at Tracy, "Well, she deserves what she gets!" 'How could a woman do that to a man?"

"No, don't turn you back on Nelly; she was just trying to survive. 'Nelly is not the same as your Ex-wife, her circumstances are completely different. 'David has been obsessed with her since she was a teenager—he was a full grown man. 'Sure it was wrong to have an affair but how long does she have to pay for her mistakes. 'She has kept her life clean for the last ten years but David never lets her forget…he still tortures her. 'If he had that much anger for her, why didn't he just divorce her? 'In the very least, he doesn't have the right to kill her… and you don't have the right to judge her," Tracy finished angrily.

Nelly jumped out of bed and ran through the open doors out to the beach. She wanted to feel something; anything; she wanted to feel the cold salty ocean burn her skin. If she could find a way to punish herself she would. Her soul was tortured. How could she have done that to David; sure he wasn't the best husband in the world but he didn't deserve what she did to him. He wouldn't be in this mess if she hadn't of had an affair or choose to run off like this. She was convinced that it changed him.

She stumbled into the edge of the gulf waters and fell into its comforting cold waves. She mixed her salty tears with the oceans own salty viscosity, her wet night shirt inappropriately stuck to her curved body making a transparent spectacle of her perfection; her actions drew the attention of others but she no longer cared. She was truly broken hearted. She did love David in her own way, it was just that things changed; David had changed. Shortly after their first child he went from the attentive loving man to something she didn't recognize. He was always mad about dinner not being on the table on time, or the crease in his pants not being stiff enough. It was no one thing that she could describe but a culmination of many things. She couldn't make mistakes because he latched onto them and yelled at her, and the baby's crying drove him crazy. He teased her when she didn't want to be teased and made a joke of her to their friends. It made her feel less than human.

She didn't notice Nick coming out of the water from his morning swim until he scooped her small body up in his strong arms and carry her back to the room where Tracy was waiting with instructions to lay Nelly on the bed. Tracy brought Nelly a drink of cold water and tried to settle her down.

"Maybe we should take her back to the hospital," Nick suggested.

"No, I know what she needs," said Tracy, "Just let her rest awhile and I'll take care of everything."

Tracy started packing her bags for *Biloxi* and signaled for a shower dampened Abby to help; meanwhile Lillian made her excuses. Lillian felt that the little group needed privacy as they worked things out; plus it felt uncomfortable to see Nick carry Nelly. Lillian wished that there was more between her and Nick. When he was around she had butterflies in her stomach and colors were sharper; she wanted to get him alone but he was always rescuing women.

"Can someone take Steve to the airport, he wants to go home," Tracy's voice was cold and icy. Abby was silent.

Steve silently finished packing and then followed Ed out into hot summer sun. Ed felt that Nelly was safe as long as she was with the ladies and Nick. As the two of them walked to the retro car, Steve felt ashamed for taking his grief for his Ex-wife out on Nelly. Tracy was right, every situation was different and everyone makes mistakes, even himself. Nelly gave him more kindness and adventure than he has ever had his lifetime; instead of thanks, he repays her with his anger; after all she was his friend and he should have stood by her.

On the way to the car, Steve tried to talk to Ed, "About Nelly…tell her…"

Before Steve could finish an angry Ed pinned Steve's shoulder against the solid sandy colored brick wall with one large hand and hissed in Steve's his face, "Look, people fall in and out of love all the time but that doesn't give a person the right to kill or maim."

Just as suddenly, Ed let go of Steve and violently smoothed his hair back while trying to shake off the anger. He turned his back to Steve as he thought David had not only threatened Nelly's life but his own.

Steve violently threw his bag down on the sidewalk and faced the ocean. He took a deep breath and with a lot of emotion in his voice, said regretfully, "I know, I SCREWED UP….I screwed up….OK… I screwed up."

"Yeah you did," Ed said as he led the rest of the way to the challenger.

CHAPTER 29

The Reveal

Ed exchanged phone numbers with Steve in case there were any other questions from the F.B.I.; that was if the F.B.I. ever showed up, he thought. He had to find out, so he dialed Jack's number.

"Hey Jack, what's going on?" Ed asked, "Where the hell is the F.B.I?"

"Just hang in there Ed, there is a jurisdiction issue. I'll let you know when you can come home," Jack promised.

"Well, we're on the way to *Biloxi*...they might want to know that if they finally get their act together," Ed said in frustration.

"Ed you can't let them go to *Biloxi*...this ain't no damn vacation," Jack lectured but Ed hung up before Jack had a chance to finish.

****

As the ocean breeze found its way inland, it blew through the leaves of the palm tree in front of the hotel where Nick stood waiting for Ed. Nick's loose Hawaiian shirt blew against his lean body like a flag waving on a pole.

When Ed arrived at the hotel, Nick called to Ed and invited him over to the side of the building to speak in private. He didn't know how to start the conversation so he simple said, "This has gotten more complicated."

"What has gotten more complicated…what are you talking about?" Ed thought that this couldn't get any more complicated.

Nick reached in his back pocket and pulled out his wallet; then displayed his private detective license. He also pulled out a court order giving him permission to follow Nelly.

"Holly shit! 'David hired you to follow Nelly." Ed assumed the worst.

"No, her father did."

Then Nick explained to a stunned Ed, "I didn't know why Mr. Durrell hired me to follow Nelly until fifteen minutes ago but apparently she is his estranged daughter. 'He is flying into *Panama City Beach* this afternoon and I'm supposed to make the introductions."

Ed kicked at something imaginary, "How many more people are going to come out of the woodworks and confess to following Nelly."

"What do you mean?" Nick asked.

"Well there was me for one, her husband for two, you for three and the F.BI. is on their way," Ed went on to fill Nick in on what happened in *Montgomery*.

Nick glanced at the gulf sea with his smooth face into the breeze causing his long black hair to blow like a windsock before he decided to confess, "It was my guy that ran into David's car at the hospital. 'I had him tailing her because I needed a break. 'Mike saw the whole thing and tried to stop David."

"He probably saved her life," Ed was grateful that Mike made his job easier.

"I'll tell you what, let's keep this between us for now. 'The girls know that I'm supposed to protect them in *Biloxi* but I think that it would be a good idea for you to make some excuse to tag along, tell them that you have always wanted to see *Biloxi*," Ed suggested.

"What about Mr. Durrell when he arrives this afternoon, can you keep the ladies here long enough for him to meet his daughter?" Nick asked.

"Mr. Durrell is a big boy, you can call him and tell him to catch up in *Biloxi*," Ed said without sympathy, "besides I think that you better talk to Nelly first rather than just spring it on her…she has already been through too much."

"Ok, well, it will make my job easier if I can work out in the open, the Impala was getting stuffy," Nick said relieved.

"Yeah, and I can use the help keeping up with the ladies."

"Why does Mr. Durrell want to find his daughter now, after all these years?" Ed suddenly wondered.

"I don't know but it seems that he ran into an old girlfriend that he hadn't seen since around Nineteen-sixty. 'Apparently she had a child of his that he didn't know about," Nick told the quick version of the story.

"We'll follow them in the Challenger. 'Can you stash your car somewhere?" Ed asked as he thought that he would ask more about this later.

"I think that would be a good idea. 'Abby had her nose up against my glass window the other night. 'If it wasn't for the tinted windows it would have been all over,'" Nick confessed a little embarrassed.

"You know, Nelly looks good for her age but she is fifty; so how old is her father?" Ed suddenly felt curious.

Nick grinned, "I've new respect for Middle aged women. 'I'm not sure if I could jump out of a moving car at my age let alone nearly fifty; Nelly must be a genetic anomaly."

Then Nick said, "I'll catch up with you in thirty minutes, I need to make a phone call."

****

The phone at the Barkowski house was at least sixty years old. It was an old black phone with a rotary dial and a larger than life ring; Mrs. Barkowski picked up the phone and listened to her son as he told the story of the shark and then about Lillian inadvertently calling him "Shark Fighter" at dinner.

When he told his mother, she wasn't all that impressed by the actual name "Shark Fighter" but she was proud that his ancestors had finally spoken to him. She was afraid that since she married outside her tribe that she might be punished by the ancestors by not accepting her child. She was the child of many generations of chiefs and the first to break the blood line.

Before they hung up, she said she would ensure that the council would consider the experience and make a judgment but that he must bring a witness so that his story could be told by another. Then the elders could create a picture of the event and ponder wisely on his new name. This would be important since he was one of the few who received his name as an adult. She would set up the event with the elders and afterwards the celebration.

As he closed his cell phone he wondered how he could convince Lillian to come home with him to be his witness. She was his only witness. How would he explain their tribal rituals and passages of rights? He liked Lillian and wondered what she would think of his people...his mother...their traditions? Also, his daughter, Star, was on his mind. He was considered her Uncle but he really wanted her to be proud of him. Should he have given her up?

He would think about all this later because right now he had a job to do.

CHAPTER 30

Mr. Durrell

Neal sat at the bar of *The Kumar Inn Beach Resort* Sunday evening and ordered a cold Miller light from the friendly bar tender. As he waited for his beer, he tapped his fingers against the bamboo edge of the teakwood counter. His back was against the ocean so he spun the swivel stool around and sat back against the counter in order to enjoy the ocean; watching the waves as they rushed to shore. When his beer arrived he sightlessly reached behind him until he could feel the cold moist bottle and wrapped his hands around it. It felt good as he guzzled the cool liquid down his throat and relieved himself with a small inaudible belch.

Earlier he had tried to find his mother but the pretty hotel clerk said that she had gone; that she would be back in a couple of days for "the wedding." She explained to him that a friend of his mother's was marrying her uncle on Saturday. Then she insisted on giving him a room justified by him being Nelly's son made him a friend of the family—and insisted that he stayed for the wedding. She said that she was terrible sorry about his father but he wasn't in the loop on the most recent event so he didn't understand any of it. All he understood was that his only choice was to stay put until his mother showed up. He hoped that he wouldn't lose his job with the impromptu vacation but he felt like he needed to find his mother first and foremost. He father seemed to be on some kind of meltdown.

Anyway, Neal hadn't been on a vacation in years so he thought that he would enjoy himself; until she returned, there was nothing else to do.

He had ripped the sleeves out of his cotton shirt and wore a pair of comfortable blue jeans. A young woman across the bar admired his pretty boy good looks and unusual golden blond hair that had the look of oxidized gold with lighter flickers of golden threads shimmering in the soft light.

An older man, looking to be in his late seventies or early eighties, but sturdy from a lifetime of hard work, sat a stool away. The elderly guy wore a large western hat, cowboy boots and a belt with a large silver buckle sporting an embossed picture of a bull. There was an interesting since of familiarity about him. Noticing Neal watching him he nodded a friendly hello and then ordered a beer.

Neal decided to start up a conversation, "excuse me sir, I have a since of familiarity toward you, do I know you from somewhere?"

"You put that quite eloquently, young man, I was feeling the same way," Mr. Durrell returned the greeting in a heavy mid-western accent.

Mr. Durrell studied the young man's unusually full lips, large blue eyes and golden hair before a startling realization came to him. This boy was the spitting image of his son. Only the boy was much younger.

"What's your name son?" Mr. Durrell asked.

"Neal…Neal McMillan…what's yours?" Neal asked as he looked into steel blue eyes and held his hand out to shake. Neal thought about the eyes, that was why he looked familiar; the old guy's eyes looked like his mothers.

Mr. Durrell's jaw dropped as he starred at the young man sitting before him. She's has a son he thought, Bill never thought to ask Nick if Nelly had children. Of course she had to have grown children, what about grandchildren? He had missed her whole life and she was not only a mother but she could be a grandmother.

Neal almost withdrew his hand before Mr. Durrell came to his senses and grabbed Neal's hand. With new gusto he shook Neal's hand vigorously and with a strong grip said, "I'm very glad to meet you son…very glad!"

Neal felt a little uncomfortable that this stranger would react so enthusiastically and had already decided to escape to his room to watch a well know street racing movie on cable TV. He was afraid to become "hung up" with the old guys corny stories. Mr. Durrell insisted on buying him another beer so being raised to be of a polite, respectful, nature to his elders, Neal decided to give the old guy a little more attention.

"Do you have any brothers or sisters?" To Neal the old man seemed much too nosey for his taste but he continued to act politely. Neal didn't think that it would hurt anything if he told a little about his family.

"Yes sir, I have a pretty sister in Nashville, Tennessee. Her name is Julia."

"Do you have pictures? Do you have any children?" Mr. Durrell begged.

"Sir, I don't believe that you mentioned your name," Neal reminded him.

"I'm sorry, I became a little carried away, my name is Bill Durrell," he apologized.

Then Bill decided to revert to a new tactic to extract information by instead talking about himself. He begin to realize he was scaring the young man away so he told Neal stories that only an old man could acquire through many years of living. He told of his ranching days and teenage folly's like going after the neighbors cows to learn how to lasso. He described the beautiful country in *Montana* and *Wyoming*, how he loved to snow mobile across the prairie; how he liked to ride four wheelers up the mountains near the glaciers and, as a child, how he loved to dig up rattle snakes. He talked about hunting Grizzlies when it was legal to hunt Grizzlies and elk, antelope, and dear.

Neal sat fascinated by his stories and enjoyed everyone, after all. Then the mood of the conversation started to change.

"A couple of years ago my son entered a bull riding contest in Casper, Wyoming. 'He did pretty good but was bucked off the bull and unfortunately the bull gored him in the gut. 'Jason fought hard to survive his injuries but, in the end, he died in the Casper Wyoming hospital. 'There wasn't anything anyone could do. 'He was our only son and he had never married, so I thought that was the end of the bloodline," William said slowly and carefully with purpose. The he paused and took a deep breath before nervously continuing, "I thought that it was the end of my world… until I found that I had a daughter I never knew about so I've come here to meet her."

As Bill told his story, there were tears in his eyes.

Neal reached out and compassionately patted Mr. Durrell on the shoulder and said, "I'm sorry about your son."

"No that's not why this old guy is a little emotional, it's just that I found out tonight that she had a son," Bill continued to confess to Neal.

Reaching into his back pocket, Mr. Durrell pulled out a wallet with a worn, wrinkled, old picture and showed it to Neal. It was of a young man in his mid twenties dressed in chaps standing next to a split rail fence covered with several saddles. To Neal it was like looking into his own face. The resemblance was startling; it was like he had a twin.

In seeing the resemblance of his new found grandson to his son, there was now no doubt in Mr. Durrell's mind that the story was true. DNA tests would not be necessary to confirm this was his grandson because the family resemblance told it all. All he needed was just an old faded photograph that mirrored his grandson to his son as if they were twins from different times and different parts of the country. The picture was twenty years old but it was of his son at the same age as Neal was now.

"OK, what's the joke here, this is almost the spitting image of myself. 'Mister, what are you trying to pull?" Neal could feel the embarrassment, shock and anger fill his face.

"It's no joke. 'I'm your biological Grandfather Neal. 'That daughter that I've followed here to meet is your mother," Mr. Durrell carefully confessed.

"Why hasn't she told me this," Neal asked still trying to absorb the shock.

"She doesn't know," He said, sad for the loss of getting to know his own child.

"Grandma had a reputation of being a…well…a party girl before she married but I would never expect she kept a secret like this, mom always said that she was a character," Neal said a little dumbfounded. "Poor Grandpa, he had to learn while he was in heaven. 'Ok, to sum this all up, I'm your estranged Grandson. 'I like you so far, so this may work out."

"Your grandpa was my best friend and being that you have my obvious family traits, I have a feeling that he knew before he died but he loved your mom too much to say anything," Mr. Durrell consoled Neal, "She was wild but she was special."

"Hey, that's my Me Maw for which you're speaking," Neal was repulsed.

Then Mr. Durrell continued, "I can't do anything about the past but I'd like to get to know you and your mom in the future. 'May I spend some time with you while I'm here?"

Neal hesitated, "I'm going to have to call Me Maw as I know she will be pretty messed up about all this but the answer is sure…I want to get to know you too."

"There is one other thing I want from you," Mr. Durrell looked hopeful.

"OK," Neal said without knowing what to expect.

"I have a ranch and several small businesses…I need a heir…would you consider coming back with me and just seeing if you would like to learn the family business?" Bill asked trying not to apply any pressure. "Together with yourself, your sister will also be welcome to share in the same offer if you will break the news to her."

"This is a lot to take in one night, can I sleep on it?" Neal didn't know why he needed time to think about it, it wasn't like he was an executive at the Express Lube.

"Sure son, in the meantime, I'll wait here in *Panama City Beach* with you while you wait on your mom that will give us some time."

CHAPTER 31

Biloxi

Nelly was wearing a long white gown that flowed so lightly in air that it looked like a graceful ghost in the night as she walked through the open doors of a veranda, which was lined with sweet scented, flowering, vines. The melody of an enchanted love song played from somewhere inside; then suddenly, before her, a gorgeous tuxedo clad man appeared holding out his right hand in a silent gesture toward an invitation to dance. She couldn't believe her eyes as the man gracefully pulled her inside his circle. With perfect formation, he glided her into a beautiful flowing waltz, swinging her in graceful circles and lifts. She was overwhelmed with happiness to be dancing so wonderfully. She felt like a butterfly spreading colorful wings to fly. Then he abandoned Nelly by stepping back into the night from which he came; replacing Nelly with another beautiful dancer in a long flowing gown taking took Nelly's place. She watched in fascination as the two of them dance away in such grace as never seen before and Nelly was overwhelmed with tears at their perfection took her breath away. Her feet felt glued to the wooden deck and the rhythm was gone.

Then as Nelly stood alone on the veranda, an anticipating fear struck the very core of her soul; she knew something was about to happen. It did as Dark shadowy demons with shining eyes begin to creep up from every direction, screaming there agony and swallowing her with her own sins and she started screaming her fear.

"Nelly…Nelly wake up… you're having a bad dream," Tracy said as she shook Nelly violently.

Nelly was covered in perspiration as she woke. "I was dreaming that demon were about to take me away to pay for my sins. 'Do you think that it happens that way?'"

"Honestly Nelly, it's not as simple as all that, it's between you and God and he forgives," Tracy tried to console Nelly.

"Anyway, we are *Biloxi* and you promised me a surprise for my bachelorette party. 'How did you get this room?' What is my/our surprise at midnight? 'It's so Cinderella-ish…or mysterious…I need to drink beer," Abby interjected excitedly as she waved her hand around to display the luxurious room.

"What time is it?" Nelly asked as she jumped out of bed and headed toward the shower.

"It's eleven thirty," Tracy offered helpfully.

"Are you guys ready? 'It will only take me a minute," Nelly called to the two women as she ran into the bathroom.

"We've been ready," Abby called after her.

Down stairs Nelly seemed to be searching for someone but settled on sitting at a raised bar in the middle of a bunch of Rolette tables; she kept stretching her neck out and looking over the heads of her two friends and then again behind her. Where was he she thought out loud but it was too noisy for anyone to hear her. Abby and Tracy looked at each other with a question on their face. What could Nelly be up to now?

At one time they heard a voice holler out from the mass of gamblers, "Hey ladies, want a date."

She thought that might be him but she didn't see anyone.

Then Nelly said, "Come on, let's go to the corner bar in the lobby called the *Gulf Night Club*." She had finally spotted him sitting along the side of the bar looking handsome in an Australian type of getup, complete with a big hat that he must have bought from overseas. She missed him because she wasn't expecting the hat.

Abby and Tracy could hardly keep up with her as she practically ran over to greet him. As they came up behind him, Nelly cleared her throat and dully said, "Hey mister…ah sir, do you want a threesome?"

He reached out like they were old friends and hugged the three of them. Tracy and Abby finally recognized him and started laughing. "You're the guy from the *McMulligan's Bar and Grill!* Nelly, you are full of surprises!"

"Yeah, but she sucks at picking up men," John laughed while doing the magic trick of pulling a chip out of Abby's ear, "Come on, you look like a bunch of Virgins to me."

"Excuse me," they all three said in unison.

"You've never gambled before," he explained, "That means that you have beginners luck."

"Oh," they said as they followed him through the *Belle Rose Casino* lobby of Rolette tables and poker machines. Voices and bells filled the air so loudly that they could hardly hear each other. The isles were so packed with people that they had to squeeze through bodies in chairs playing one arm bandits; there was a group of beautiful perfectly shaped women in skimpy pastille outfits and obviously augmented breasts standing in one of the carpeted isles.

John nodded toward them and yelled, "There is a golf convention this week and the Bunny's were invited."

"That's real cool!" Abby hollered over the sounds as she thought this couldn't be a more perfect bachelorette party.

"Oh Lord, I forgot about Ed," Tracy said as she suddenly remembered that she was supposed to let him know if they went anywhere.

"Forget him, his probably sleeping like a baby and he needs it," Abby suddenly felt like they were teenagers again skipping school for a party.

"We'll catch up with him later," Nelly promised.

John stopped at a poker machine and handed the girls some chips. "Ya' all try your luck."

Everyone but Nelly held back as they realize that there was considerable amount of money put into the chips that he handed them. It didn't seem right to blow someone else's money, let alone a practical stranger's. Nelly excitedly poked the money into the slot and pushed the button, she chose two's wild.

It must have taken one-hundred dollars before Nelly decided his advice was bad and told him that, "well I might suck at picking up men but you suck at gambling." Then she ran over to the Rolette table with the other three in tow and, with the advice of a sweet little lady from India whose husband was playing, laid her chips on a series of numbers. John and the ladies were cheering her on as she doubled John's three hundred dollars in thirty minutes.

"It seems that pretty little ladies from India are good luck to me and better gamblers than you," she told both the lady and John while remembering Lillian giving them a room.

After Nelly gave the Indian lady fifty dollars for her advice, she gave John back his three-hundred dollars in chips and pocketed around two-hundred-forty-five. Then given the hour, Nelly invited John back to their room for a drink. Abby and Tracy politely returned their unspent chips and agree that it was time to go back to the room too.

"Let's get some booze first," John said cheerfully.

"OK, I'll go with you," Abby was an expert regarding beer and wanted to insure that he did it right.

Abby and John ran off to the Quick Trip for beer and wine while Tracy and Nelly returned to the room. Tracy stopped to knock on Ed's room but changed her mind. She missed Ed and wanted to spend more time with him. It was too soon to tell but they seemed to have something special. She thought about Daniel, her ex-husband, he seemed so far away. She hadn't thought about him in days and that had never happened since the divorce.

When John and Abby returned they were laughing hysterically. At first the joke seemed private but after a few minutes Abby was about to bust to tell Nelly and Tracy the antics of John.

They opened the drapes to let in the street lights from below and Tracy poured a glass of wine into a plastic water glass; meanwhile John and Abby broke into a bottle of beer; Nelly stuck to her water.

"We walked by a bunch of those Bunnies's while coming back to the hotel... well John preceded to pull his pants down and moon them," Abby laughed hysterically.

"Well how was it?" a laughing Nelly asked Abby.

"What," Abby looked confused.

"Well, his butt of course, how was it?" Nelly laughed.

Abby kissed her fingers and fanned them out like a gourmet cook who just approved of her own meal, "Magnificent, just ask the Bunny's, they agreed!"

"Oh, let's judge for ourselves," Tracy teased John.

"Well, ladies, I'm drunk, same place, different time tomorrow?" John said as he bi-stepped the mooning demonstration.

"I'm glad you hooked with him, he is so much fun," Abby congratulated Nelly after John left.

CHAPTER 32

David on the Run

It was along the bend of a North Georgia mountain road when the breaks gave out. David fought a good battle in keeping the car on the road, but the sharp curve was so that even the best of drivers couldn't easily negotiate going at ninety-miles an hour. Throughout it all, he immediately knew that that he was racing over the edge of the mountain to his death. His life with Nelly flashed before him; he loved her and wanted to live long enough to make all this right again. He knew what he did was wrong and if he lived through this he would turn himself in to face the consequences. She just made him crazy with her independence but he would learn to live with it. He was thinking all this as the car sliced through the mettle guards to careen off the road down the face a 150-foot drop.

Somehow time slowed down long enough for David to think of his wife and to say a quick prayer. Please watch over my wife and children, he prayed, and forgive my sins. Then he prayed for God to perform a miracle and put love and forgiveness in Nelly's heart. She was good women and he now realized that the circumstances of their marriage was unusual, and nobody's fault. He forgave her then and there.

The car bounced and made horrible crunching and moaning sounds as it catapulted down the side of Mountain, impacting against every rock and tree in its way.

Unmercifully, David survived with tormenting pain coming from a broken pelvis and fractured arm. Every part of his injured body hurt as he hung upside down from his seat belt at the bottom of the ravine. Using his good arm he felt around for his car phone; he fought to stay conscious and somewhere in the back of his mind was grateful that he had lived through his ordeal. He would get help and make it up to his family. That was his last thought as the damaged gas tank of the little Honda ignited to erupt in a large explosion that burned trees for yards around.

CHAPTER 33

Biloxi night

Monday night, after a day of good food, good shopping and long napping, John rang the room about nine p.m. to invite the ladies out to dinner and dancing. Ed and Nick had worn themselves out following the women all day and had again retired early; with the expectation that the women would do the same. However, again the women snuck out to meet John at the *Gulf Bar* where a wonderful Oldies band of elderly nice looking black men called *The Sun Beams* was playing. The dance floor was bustling with vacationers enjoying the good music. Four of the Playboy Bunny's sat in a booth nearby curiously watching the older women dance.

They all took turns dancing with John, but Tracy thought that later she would even the number a little and go back to get Ed and Nick. However, John didn't need help; he was a bundle of energy and danced well with all three women. Plus, they were asked by others to dance so Tracy wouldn't bother Ed for right now.

As the group went back to their cozy circular booth, against Nelly's protests, John ordered Nelly a margarita.

Nelly had on maxi style light tan dress with clear sequences that shimmered in the soft lights as she danced and Tracy wore a pretty summery number with a white bolero. They had just bought the dresses that day at a quaint dress shop in the hotel shopping mall. Meanwhile, Abby still sported her usual blue jeans and t-shirt.

The *Belle Rose Casino* was everything that they imagined it to be and more. The marble floors shined with polish, the gardens were well manicured and the entertainment was limitless.

"I don't drink," Nelly protested.

"Darlin, It's not going to hurt you, so chug-a-lug," John order her with humor.

"Alright, just one…mmmmm…that's like drinking desert," Nelly complimented his choice of a margarita and ordered another.

"Hell it ain't enough, you need a buzz" he said noticing that it didn't affect her that much so he ordered her a shot of tequila.

"I'll get drunk and make a fool of myself," she protested.

"Nope, I won't let you, I just want you to drink enough to think I'm a good dancer," he smiled.

"I already think you're a good dancer, so do the Bunny's in the corner booth over there, they haven't taken their eyes off of you all night," she smiled back while remembering that he mooned them.

They showed Nelly how to lick the salt off the back of her hand and then chug down the shot of tequila. After two shots she was feeling well enough to dance. She danced with a young black man, keeping up with his bumping and grinding like a pro. He moved his hand down her face and body; while she nearly went to the floor with her squirming. There was something about that that made John protective so he decided to drag the women out on the beach where he could have them to himself. They were all slightly sauced and together in unison sang *"Under the Boardwalk," by the Rolling Stones* while walking down the sidewalk in the warm summer air in front of a well lit, bigger than life, *Belle Rose Casino* entrance. Nelly turned to Tracy and slurred a complimented, "Girl you can really sing well."

"You're drunk," Tracy laughed, "But so am I."

While trying to get to the ocean they decided to cross the off ramp to the expressway; meanwhile car lights beaming in their eyes and horns honked all around them. The alcohol had put a dampener on their ability to sense the danger in strolling amongst freeway traffic—but finally they came to the safety of a large cement medium for which they all stumbled over and fell into a pile on the soft sand. They removed their shoes and continued on to the beach.

"I believe that we could take that walkway behind the hotel on the way back, rather than play in traffic," Nelly suggested as she pointed to the wooden decked walkway.

"Shit, I didn't see that," John found it funny now but later would panic at the thought of putting these precious ladies lives in danger.

"Let's all go skinny dipping!" Tracy teased, "I want to see John's butt."

"Ok, you first Tracy," John was excited to see naked women.

"No, you first," Tracy countered with a hopeful grin.

Then Nelly did what no one expected, she pulled off her dress and threw it up in the air. The ocean breeze caught the dress like a kite and carried it like shimmering angel wings down the beach. John, Tracy and Abby starred at the dress as it floated in its ghostly dance against the backdrop of bright stars ten feet above their heads and then flew away. They were too busy to notice Nelly take her bra off and see a pair of perfect breasts bounce as she ran into the waves of the gulf, falling clumsily into its salty kelp filled water.

"Wow, that looked like it was in a movie," Abby offered but John and Tracy were now staring at a half naked Nelly with their jaws dropped.

Tracy jumped up and ran after Nelly's dress to cover her before anyone saw her. They were right there near the expressway and Nelly could get arrested for indecent exposure.

After Nelly dressed, John looked up at the sky, breathed in and said, "This is the most amazing night."

He jumped up and took turns dancing with all three women, one at a time as they laughed and sang.

"Well, ladies all good things must come to an end," John said with a yawn, "I've got meetings in the morning but I'll see you tomorrow night, if you still want to play some more."

Nelly was sobering up as she realized that this was only one side of John, the other side must be extremely serious.

"Of course," Abby agreed, "It's my bachelorette party, and I wouldn't miss it for the world."

John looked at Nelly with a question in his eyes.

"Abby here is in an arranged marriage," Nelly volunteered.

"Wow, that sucks," John responded.

"I'm happy, look all I get," as she said that, they all assumed that she meant a rich husband because nothing was ever mentioned to them about Christopher buying her *Aviation World*. Having a rich husband would never be enough but the revenge of seeing everyone's faces as she walked into the doors as their new owner was enough.

When they arrived back in the room at two a.m. they found Ed and Nick waiting for them. Ed was obviously furious.

"Where have you all been?" Ed demanded.

"Ed it's my fault, I wanted to show Abby a good time for her Bachelorette party, we were just downstairs," Nelly apologized.

Ed ran his fingers through his hair, he was disappointed that they didn't come get him and he was worried about Nelly. The phone had rung at Midnight with the news about how David had died in a car accident. He didn't know how to tell Nelly as she was already thinking that she was going to hell and blaming herself for David's actions. The F.B.I was finally in the picture but they were in *North Georgia* investigating the scene of the accident. They wanted Nelly back in Atlanta for questioning as soon as possible but he knew that she would only cooperate to an extent. She felt responsible for her friends return home.

"Nelly, please, they've found David and he was in an accident…Nelly, he is dead," Ed said carefully.

She stood frozen in the middle of the room not knowing what to do. Nick tried to hold her up but she yelled at him to get back, and started screaming that it was all her fault and all she wanted to do was die.

"It's my entire fault, I should be the one that died…it's not fair, it's my entire fault!" she cried. Then she gathered herself together and asked twice, "What's next? 'What's next?"

"Nelly, you have to go back to Atlanta tomorrow to meet with the FBI. 'You've done nothing illegal but they have a lot of questions before they close the case," Ed explained.

"Back to Atlanta? 'Oh Lord, what will I tell the children?' What about the wedding?" she was in shock.

"I'm afraid that you will miss that, the F.B.I. will not want you to leave town until everything is sewed up," he said sadly. "In the morning, I'll follow Tracy and Abby back to *Panama City Beach* in your car so they can get home after the wedding and you have a ticket waiting for you at the Gulfport Airport. 'The F.B.I will pick you up in *Atlanta*."

Nelly ran out of the room and back down the elevator to the lobby, still lively at three in the morning. She bellied up to the bar and ordered another shot of tequila like a pro. No one dared follow her as they knew that she needed time alone. They also knew that she was a tough lady; she didn't need to prove that she wouldn't somehow get through this. Next to her at the bar was a young geeky looking man with a laptop who sat drinking a beer and typing away as he noticed Nelly flop down beside him.

"Miss, I don't mean to pry but you look troubled," the man looked genuinely concerned while he pushed up a heavy set of glasses with his index finger.

"Ah, it's just me, I seem to get in trouble everywhere I go lately," she said, both not wanting to offend or burden him with her troubles.

"You have some pretty hair there lady," he complimented.

"Thanks, what are you doing on that laptop?" Nelly asked, distracted by the computer.

"Oh, my uncle has me under pressure to finish an inventory program for a sales pitch to some of the government contractors with which he is in contact. 'Their program is old and cumbersome. 'They need something more accurate to help with better tracking of military funds and for balancing the budget, times are hard for the president," he sounded frustrated. "My uncle is a hell-of-a-guy that will try just about anything to make money but I think that he has me taking on more than I can chew."

Nelly thought, why not, she would never use her computer program anyway, she wasn't even interested in it anymore, plus no one would take her serious unless she just gave it away. It was worth a try to help this poor kid.

"Here, are you connected to the internet," she asked as she reached for his computer.

"Yes," he said a little leery about letting her use his computer. There were some pretty sensitive programs linked to it.

She typed in remote URL address to her server and showed the computer geek the inventory program that she written, it was nice to meet someone of the same spirit for a change. "Look she said you have to consider all aspects of the program from inventory to an accounting standpoint, from tracking piece parts or supplies, to labor, inventory of parts and I've even added enough room to automatically create direct links to the Original Manufactures Technical Data for direct downloading. All you have to do is to just type in the link and the pass word and it remembers it. She went on to explain, "You can print reports here and maintain security passwords here."

She showed him more aspects to her program and then gave a complete stranger the password to her server where she stored her program. She said that he could access it and download whatever he wanted.

"Just take the program, it's yours if you can use it, and adjust it to your needs, I'll never use it," she said as she swallowed down another shot of tequila.

"This is easy, the links are set up like a flow chart which guides you step-by-step, I like it, Thanks!" he sounded like a big weight was taken off of his shoulders.

They sat there for another two hours customizing the program to what he thought that the government contractors needed before Nelly felt too exhausted to continue. She was grateful for the distraction but it was time to get a little rest before she leaves for Atlanta in the morning. She was numb inside and too drunk to care.

"Lady, I don't know what I would have done without you, I had been working on this project for nine for weeks, you're a genius, it makes my program look like a first grader created it," he said as he shook her hand.

"What's your name, I'll be sure that you get some credit for this," he asked.

"Nelly McMillan, but don't worry about it, it was just a hobby for me and I'm glad someone appreciates it, heaven knows—I'll never get anywhere with it," she said before staggering off to her room.

As she went back to her room for some much needed rest, she ran into the four Bunny's that were in the bar that evening.

"Hi Miss," one of them greeted her, "We've been watching you all weekend and we just wanted to say how proud we are of you and your friends. ' It seems like most old people these days just get lazy and never enjoy themselves…and the gentleman is such a good looking bugger."

"Well thank you, I'll take that as a complement, even if you did just call me old," Nelly wasn't in real good humor.

Nelly went back to the room where everyone was sound asleep; even Nick and Ed were asleep in the chairs. She dug through her purse and found her cell phone. She hadn't paid attention to it in days and the messages were backed up. She swallowed a lump in her throat as she saw David's messages. Instead of listening to them she deleted them all so that the F.B.I couldn't find them and then stepped out on the balcony to call Neal, Julia and her Mother-in-law Janice. They needed to know about David.

In a sleepy haze Neal answered his phone, "Mom, I've tried to reach you for days. 'Dad is looking for you."

"Neal honey, your Dad was in an accident, he is dead," Nelly said softly.

"Oh God no, does Julia know about this?"

"No dear, can you call her and let her know that we are all meeting at the house in Atlanta," Nelly started to cry.

"Mom, one other thing I need to tell you," Neal said but then thought it wasn't the time, "Never mind, I'll tell you in Atlanta." He had a lot to deal with right now as he loved his father.

CHAPTER 34

Weddings in the Family

As Abby turned back and forth, admiring herself in the full length mirror, she thought it seemed odd to be wearing Hindu Wedding garments at a Catholic wedding. They called her wedding gown a Sari but true to Christopher's word a pair of red colored silk britches was sewed with delicate gold brocade sewed thickly around the waist and around the pant legs. The matching top showed her bare waist but a red scarf, called a chunri, with gold inlay was tucked into her waistband and draped over one shoulder to cover her entire outfit to ensure her modesty. On her head she wore a crown and a red veil that reached her waist; and long dangling earrings adorned her ears. She had gold chains draped across her forehead with a red bangle dripping down the center. She also had gold chains around her ankle and around her wrists. The makeup was thick around her eyes, enhancing their lovely gray color. A small design of the crown on her head was painted in sandalwood on her cheek. Her full lips were painted a lovely red and her cheeks were slightly naturally pink from excitement.

In this get up, she felt both feminine and like an idiot at the same time but it was a small price to pay to own *Aviation World*. Plus, Christopher was not a bad looking guy and maybe an arranged marriage would work for her. She'd be well looked after and she already loved the family, even

Granny. She just wished she had more time to get to know everyone before the marriage but Granny said it was the Indian way.

The antique church was filled with red roses and guests from all over the world. The prince of Kawate wore a full military uniform and several other guests had the look of diplomats. Some seemed puzzled that Granny would set her son up with an American but she was a wise woman so they would respect her. She also had money in everyone's pockets so no one questioned her decisions.

Tracy and Lillian proceeded Abby as her Brides Maids and, while Abby entered, the whole church stood. Abby could do nothing but stare at Christopher who looked very handsome in his traditional white brocade silk suit with a turban on his head, and a sword at his side. When he saw his bride he removed his turban to symbolizing the American tradition of removing your hat indoors for the woman you respect. She was touched by that as his thick black but slightly salted hair was uncovered for his American wife. His dark skin glowed in the light of the stain glass cross. In one short week, Abby had bypassed dating and married one of the wealthiest men in the south, and she now realized that he was quite a catch, even without the money. If it wasn't for Nelly this would have never happened. How she wished Nelly could have been here but the F.B.I. and David's funeral tied her up.

Catholic weddings were long and ritualistic but very romantic as couple's promises were made before God for a lifetime. The reception was held on the mansion lawn amongst the mimosa trees, giant zinnias and water fountains—it lasted for hours. The food was foreign but delicious with plenty of curry chicken, rice and sweet cakes. Linen covered tables and red roses were placed everywhere and there was a band with a dance floor where the new couple led in the first dance. The cake was simple but elegant and enough for the hundreds of guests that attended. *The Kumar Inn Beach Resort* was full.

Nick turned his business over to Mike so he could attend the wedding and hang by Lillian's side. They danced together all afternoon under the supervision of Granny.

When all the guests had cleared a team of servants supervised by Granny helped open the wedding presents to see that no one insulted the new bride with something as mundane as a toaster. At Indian weddings, the gifts were never household gifts but jewels and, in this case, one person even sent a Mercedes. Granny had two stenographers writing thank you notes immediately after the gifts were opened. The opening of gifts took well into the night and Christopher, impatience for his bride, kept asking if they could do this tomorrow.

"Patience," Granny yelled and giggle, "This has to be done." However, Granny was secretly pleased that he accepted her choice of Abby for his new bride and that he couldn't wait to bed her; meanwhile, a worldly Abby actually blushed for the first time in years.

After all the gifts were open, Christopher called for his lawyer to present one more gift to Abby, "As I promised, you hold more than fifty percent of the sock in *Aviation World* and have full control over the stock holding company."

Abby spontaneously jumped out of her chair and hugged Christopher for his gift, and they finally kisses as he sat her on his lap.

"Stop that you two, I will have none of that outside the bedroom, unless you give me babies," Granny laughed.

"Babies," Abby stopped for a minute, "I've never had a child and almost forty is much too old for children."

"I'm too old for Babies too, Granny," Christopher explained.

"Nonsense, women can have babies well into their forties," she insisted.

For their Honeymoon, they went on an around the world trip and cruise for several months staying in hotel from the *Paris Hillcrest* to small Bed and Breakfasts. Abby fell in love with Christopher's adventuresome spirit and love of beautiful things. Then one day they received a message that they were to come back immediately for Lillian's arranged marriage to a doctor who was going to work at *The Kumar Medical Center*.

"I thought that she wasn't going to arrange anymore marriages?" Abby questioned Granny's sanity again.

"Apparently as it turns out, Nick Barkowski was also a doctor, as well as a private detective, and had decided to go back into practice. 'Granny wants him to run her medical center. 'She has always wanted another doctor in the family," they both couldn't wait to pack. Abby remembered when Nelly called from Atlanta to tell her that Nick was in the black Impala the night that she nosed up to its window, they had a good laugh about that. She also told Abby the whole story of Nick following her for her father Bill Durrell and how her children had gone to Wyoming with him.

To Nick it was a proud moment when he was accepted by both families, his own and Lillian's. Under the proud eyes of his mother, the council finally named him "Man who swims with Sharks." It seemed like a silly name to him but it was important to his mother so he would wear it with pride. Lillian was impressed with the ceremony as she had always like family rituals and she loved his niece; although, she couldn't quite understand the relationship until Nick explained it to her.

Lillian's wedding went off without a hitch and, this time, Nelly was able to attend.

CHAPTER 35

Back to Aviation World

Six months later, throughout the grey halls of *Aviation World* the rumors were passing from one person to another. The business was bought out by new investors who were taking the time to learn the business before meeting with the old owners. Contracts were drawn up to keep the owners in place for a several years until everything could be safely transferred and to ensure that the company didn't go belly up. Expert analysts were hired to give advice to the new owners as ownership was transferred. Abby wanted to do right by Christopher's gift by ensuring that the company not only stayed afloat but built a higher profit margin.

As Abby walked in the lobby with Christopher, she wondered what everyone would think of her very pregnant body. The doctor said that she was carrying twin boys and that the amnioceteses required for her age had read that they were in perfect health. She knew the receptionist as Susan and Susan immediately stood up to hug her.

"Abby, I heard that you were married, is this your husband," she asked excitedly not used to Abby being dressed up.

She proudly patted her stomach, "Yes, and with babies on the way."

"Oh my gosh, twins?" Susan said as she patted Abby's stomach for luck.

Christopher didn't like anyone patting the stomach of his wife and frowned while leading Abby away to the door.

"Can you open the door and let ups in," Abby asked, "Also, let Jamison and Steele know that we are here."

"Oh, I can't bother the owners," Susan said horrified.

"Abby is the new owner," Christopher said impatiently and with authority.

Susan's mouth hung open as she pressed the button. Then she gathered herself together before saying, "Ah, Sir…Mam, everyone is awaiting in the conference room and your office is ready."

"Our advisors will be here in a minute, Susan, can you show them back," she smiled at Christopher, remembering what he said about her taking charge and showing confidence.

Upon entering the building she first waddled back to Tracy's cube for a visit. Christopher politely found the break room so that he could have privacy while he waited.

"Tracy!" Abby hugged her old friend.

"Oh my Gosh, aren't you the pregnant one, you look great!" Tracy hugged her back.

"A ring?" Abby asked Tracy while noticing her ring finger.

"Yes, Ed and Me never worked out, too much distance but I did finally remarry my Ex," she said excitedly.

Abby was floored and really didn't approve, but it wasn't up to her.

"Come with me, I have a surprise for you," Abby said as she drug Tracy though the halls toward the conference room just as her assistant Timothy Ingram came through the lobby door.

Adam came out to shake the hands of the one who he thought to be the new owner when he noticed Abby. He didn't say anything but did feel uncomfortable. What was she doing her, along with Nelly, she had given her resignation.

They all walked down to the conference room where both of the old owners sat in anticipation while flanked by all the company supervisors. Tim Ingram, who would be Abby's representative from now on, reached out and shook everyone's hands.

As Abby and Christopher entered the room, Adam begun to protest that this was a private meeting but Tim spoke up ahead.

"Gentlemen, I believe that you know the new owner of your company, as she used to work here. She now owns more than fifty-one percent of the stock in both the company and the holding companies," Tim said professionally.

As jaws dropped, Tim Ingram continued by pushing packages neatly clasped together in clear plastic folders in front of everyone, "This packet outlines our business plan for the company; it consists of immediate goals and long term goals."

Tracy didn't see it coming, along with everyone else she was in shock, yet she was happy for Abby.

"Ok, Mrs. Kumar will explain the immediate terms," Tim said as he turned it over to Abby. As Abby hesitated, Christopher nodded at Abby to give her a vote of confidence. She had been preparing for this moment for months and he wanted her to realize that she was in charge.

"Yes, we've looked at forty-three businesses in the aviation field and my analysts came up with the best way we believe that this company can stay afloat during these hard economical times. I've noticed that we made less than two percent last year and I feel that we can increase that by cutting the sales team in half, and by adding less expensive customer service representatives to take their place. 'I want every sales person that makes commission to be on the road half the year meeting quotas for new customers and new contracts. 'Many of our customers are overseas and to accommodate the time difference, I will hire two new customer service representatives to work from their homes in the evenings answering the phones and maintaining our new online live chat options. 'We have a new I.T. contract to maintain our computer programs and we are looking at a new inventory program that includes bar coding for inventory purposes, created by our own Nelly McMillan. 'People we are a team here, I will not tolerate ownership of any jobs or of any customers obtained in the name of this company. 'Always remember that you work for this company, the company does not work for you. 'Raises will be based on your productivity."

"Also would someone please bring Steve into this meeting?" Nelly paused for a minute to wait until Steve arrived and then indicated for Tim to take over.

Tim took the controls again, "Gentlemen, if Steve will agree, he is to be the company's new liaison representing our new division which will be installing glass cockpits. 'Mrs. Kumar has also bought a hanger near the airport for this purpose. 'It is the wave of the future so as the glass cockpit business grows, more existing employees will be trained and transferred to the new hanger," Tim added.

Steve nodded speechless still confused as to why Abby was in charge.

"Also, Tracy you will be given a raise and go with Steve to oversee the support operations. 'Oh yes, Mrs. Kumar has also indicated that she wants to ensure everyone understands that our operations depend on the ability of the technicians to repair parts, the rest of the staff will be considered support personnel . 'One other thing, we will also hire an approved Designated Engineering Representative from the F.A.A. to manage the technical data department so we can contract out his services in order to obtain hard to buy technical data. 'It will give us leverage where Component Manuals are concerned. 'That's all for now, just read your packets and we'll meet again for questions? 'Any discussion" Tim said as he closed his book and took out a blank note book to take notes.

As they left the room so the new terms could be discussed more in depth with Tim, Christopher bumped Abby shoulder with a love tap. "That's my girl, well planned and your guy Tim is good."

"I love you," Abby said as she reached up and kissed him on the cheek. She realized all along that, that in her heart, she didn't really want revenge; she just wanted to do the right thing for her former co-workers. In ignorance the company had gotten out of control with power hungry mongrels. Christopher had taught her that having good fortune meant having humility toward responsibility; that God chooses leaders, so be fair and thankful to him.

"Hey, are you ready to drive my monster truck at the rally to night," Nelly asked Christopher. "I wish I could but I better take care of these sweet little monsters growing inside of me."

"I am looking forward to it, and you can drive next year," he smiled back. After all these years of being a widower, he was blessed with a fine wife, new experiences and two new sons on the way. No man could ask for anything more.

"Christopher, you're going to have to tell me about your first wife sometime," Abby begged as they crawled into the Mercedes.

"There is nothing to tell, I only met her once and that was at our wedding. 'She refused to come to the United States and then, one day I heard that she died of a fever."

She looked at him seriously, "Don't get hurt at the monster rally tonight, OK?"

"That's a promise," He laughed, and then he asked, "You said that you have one more person in which to say goodbye to, who is that?"

She reached down on the floor board of the Mercedes and Picked up Joe's ashes, "My first love… I want to set him free…poor guy has been in the back of my truck for years?"

Suddenly he understood.

****

As Tracy and Steve left the meeting, Steve stopped in the hall and turned to Tracy, "Oh I know now, a wild mustang."

"You crazy thing, you thought about that after all this time," Tracy laughed.

CHAPTER 36

Nelly

Nelly sat home at her dining table with a cup vanilla flavored coffee thinking about how lonely she felt for her children to be nearby. She had met her biological father whom with which she was very impressed. He dressed charmingly like a cowboy but yet he was strong and well spoken. Like any good father would normally do, he supported her throughout David's funeral; it was as if he had known her all his life. After the F.B.I. investigation, Bill had made all the funeral arrangements and hired lawyers to make sure that Nelly received a widow's pension from David's old job at the Airlines. Bill listed the condo with a real-estate agent to make a quick sale and paid the last two years of the mortgage on the house in Atlanta. Along with Nelly's children, he begged Nelly to come join him at his home in Casper Wyoming, promising her a good life with him.

In the end, Neal went with Bill, now Grandfather to him, humbled and gratefully to learn the family business—and so did Julia and her family. However, this was home for Nelly. This was the home of her church and her friends. Tracy called often but she was busy reacquainting herself with her Ex-husband.

Nelly thought about their conversation on the road concerning their fantasies and goals. In reality, most of her friend's fantasies did come true, in their own ways. First Steve got to fly in a small aircraft and sing in front of a crowd, then Tracy remarried her Ex-husband and Abby not only had a three-some but had a four-some…the twins made four. She started to feel better about the trip. At first she blamed herself for the death of David but as time pressed on she begin to forgive herself—and realized that it was meant to be—the changes cause by their adventure gave her friends a good life.

David constantly looped through her mind. She realized that David and she had problems long before her affair and it wasn't just that she didn't treat him right—but that they didn't treat each other right. But even still, as she tried to convince herself that it wasn't her fault that he accidently drove himself off of a cliff, she would always feel guilty. She wondered if he would still be alive if she would have come home, instead of driving off to *Panama City Beach*. To this, Neal wisely said that her only fault was that she should have left him years ago but then again "love has no boundaries." It was the simplest explanation as to why they stayed together, love has no boundaries—and life is full of surprises—as David himself often said "it is what it is."

Just then the doorbell rang over and over again. Nelly put her coffee down on the table and while uttering "damn kids," she ran to the door still in her pajama pants. As she opened the door she saw the last person she expected framed bigger than life by the door frame and as handsome as ever. He worn a big grin and had a red dress draped over one arm.

"What the heck…how did you know where I lived," Nelly asked.

John smiled and pushed himself through the door while saying sarcastically, "And it's nice to see you too."

"Ok, well, come in and would you like a cup of coffee," she asked politely while leading him to the kitchen.

"Nah, I got other plans," he refused while taking a crumpled piece of paper out of his pocket and handing it to her.

"What's this?" she asked a little put out by his refusal for coffee.

"Read it and you'll find out," he commanded and then smiled impishly while throwing the dress on the kitchen table.

"One-hundred and fifty dollars…I mean one hundred point five million dollars…what's this for," she said as she saw her name on the bottom of the check. "I can't take this."

He grabbed the check from her and stuck it under the *Panama City Beach* souvenir magnet on the stainless steel refrigerator, "I'm afraid that I'm not just giving you the check, I'm paying you for services rendered so you can't sue me."

"What in the hell are you talking about?" she asked irritated.

"Do you have a pair of scissors," he asked preoccupied while helping himself to searching kitchen drawers—then spotted a pair of shears in the knife holder on her kitchen cupboard.

"Sit down in the chair there a minute and let me explain," he said as she thought that maybe he would take her invitation for coffee after all.

As she sat down in the chair, he quickly grabbed her hair with a huge hand and wacked it off at the neckline with three big clips of his newly found shears. She got up and screamed at him, "Are you a mad man, you cut all my beautiful hair off."

"I think you look better in shoulder length hair, I've wanted to do that since I met you," he laughed.

"You're mean to do that, you have no right, you men are all alike, get out of my house!" she yelled at him.

"Oh honey, you've probably been wanting to cut your hair off for years, your husband was why you grew it long, am I not right?" he hit the nail right on the head as he took the long beautiful strains, stuffed them in a manila envelope and wrote the name *Locks for Love*. Nelly thought, come to think of it growing her hair long started as a habit because her husband hated her in hair short. She always wore short hair before she met him.

"Anyway, it took me awhile to find you. My geeky nephew said that you were the one behind the inventory program that we sold to the government contractors at the convention. 'You never mentioned that you were a damn computer geek," he said thoughtfully as he put the shears back.

"I didn't know that was your nephew," she countered still feeling putout about her long hair.

"We've also got more contractors in the private sector interested in your program and there is more money where that came from, that's just your first payment. '*Aviation World,* your old company, is one of the companies interested," he confessed.

She had to admit that this man, even though he was an ego maniac and assumed too much, was interesting. Life would never be boring around him.

"Ok, well thanks," she responded coldly, "now please leave."

"Go get dressed, young lady, we are going out to dinner to celebrate," he demanded again nodding at the red dress out to her.

"I'm not going anywhere with you," she cussed him back.

"Remember I've seen you half naked and I don't mind doing it again, I'll dress you myself if you don't go get dressed," he threatened.

"Alright, I'll be right back," anything to get him out of her house. She thought that she would dress and chase him out the door first so she could lock him out.

He was way ahead of her and, with a knowing gleam in his eye, offered for her to go first, "After you sweet heart."

She looked across the street at a usually empty field but now occupied by a small helicopter and wondered why she didn't hear it land. "Just where we are going out to dinner," she asked as she eyed the helicopter.

"New York, Atlanta doesn't have a restaurant that compares to the Restaurants in New York, I have a plane waiting at the airport but we've got to hurry," he said as he picked her up like a rag doll and tucked her to the helicopter. Then taking his place in the pilot seat, he turned on switches.

"You're a pilot too, Oh my Gosh, get me out of here," she started to jump out but he had already begin lifted off.

"Hang on to your life, your under the control of John Henderson and company," he teased.

She thought a minute and yelled over the sound of the blades of the cherry red Eurocopter, "I don't think that I ever knew your last name."

"Well you better get familiar with it," he grinned back.

CHAPTER 37

Three Years Later

Aviation World's profit margin had gone up from two percent to ten percent and the business plan put in place by Abby was brilliant. Work processes were improved and raises were implemented, finally bringing the technicians wages up to industry standards. Everyone worked as a team toward saving money, and everyone's opinion was important.

As for Steve the glass cockpit business took off and he was busier than he could ever imagine, but there was one more thing he felt that he must do. The day he hurt Nelly always played in the back of his mind and he wanted to apologize for it. If it wasn't for the sudden impulsive decision of the four of them to take off to *Panama City Beach*, and the braveness of Nelly to overcome the odds, all this would never have happened.

As he walked through the yard of Nelly's new Atlanta home, he stepped over a big wheels, several small toy trucks and a beat up doll. He thought that Nelly must have a grandchild visiting and wondered if he should come back later but then knew that he would lose his nerve if he left now. He noticed that the front doors were clear stain glass with abstract patterns on them and as he rang the door bell two young dark headed children shown through the glass. As they opened the door he saw that they were two beautiful oriental children probably ages four and five, a boy and girl; meanwhile an older silver headed man in his eighties followed up behind.

"You know better than to open doors to strangers," their adopted Grandfather scolded.

"Yes, sir," they said as they ran off.

"Can I help you son?" Bill asked as Allison stuck her head out from around the corner of the kitchen to see who it was. The older woman was covered with a lacy apron.

"Who is it dear?" Allison asked and Bill waved her back to the kitchen. Supper smelled wonderful and he didn't want her distracted from it. Since he retired and turned the business over to his Grandchildren, visiting his daughter and good cuisine was about his two most favorite pleasures in life. He wasn't about to let this stranger distract him from his supper.

"Well?"

"I'm Steve Jones, one of Nelly's old friends, is she around?" he hesitated at the word friend.

"Sure, she is in the back yard watering the vegetable garden, come on in," the old guy suddenly became a lot friendlier.

When Steve saw her for the first time in three years, he thought that she was just as beautiful as she ever was. Her hair was a little shorter but it looked good.

"Fight with any alligators lately?" he asked in his distinctly recognizable low toned voice as he crept up on her.

She dropped her hose, turned around and jumped up on him and gave him a big hug, "I'm so glad to see you!"

"So this means I'm forgiven?" he asked and then he couldn't help himself as he stared into her lovely eyes, he had to kiss her, something he had wanted to do for three years.

He wrapped his arms around her and hungrily pressed his lips against the softness of her lips, while caressing the small of her back. He picked her up and held her closer and pressed her ample breasts against his chest. Then he reluctantly pushed her away. While trying to remember himself, he slowing stepped back.

A CHANGE OF LUCK

"I'm sorry, I didn't mean to do that, it's just that I've wanted to do that for a long time," he confessed.

She stepped closer and softly joked, "So have I, every since *Panama City Beach* when I saw your six pack."

"I thought that you were involved with that John…Henderson was his name?" he asked.

She deepened her voice to mimic her Wyoming father's voice, "Trying to hold on to John was like trying to hold on to a wild bobcat. 'You can feed it and love it but the only thing that makes it happy is to turn it loose. Anyway, that's what my father said."

"I'm glad you have another character in your life to mimic," Steve laughed, "Who are the cute kids and the old man?" He asked this while watching the children and the old guy peak at them through the window.

"My kids, actually John and I adopted them from China; that was before we divorced over a year ago. 'I can afford to give them a good home," she said lovingly, "The old guy is my biological father, I'm sure you heard about him."

"I'm glad about the kids, it suits you to be an adopted mom," Steve complimented.

"They still love John but he is more like a jolly old uncle to them," she added thinking that she never wanted to exclude John from their lives. He was a good man, but Nelly believed that her father was right about John never settling down. "Plus, we have a nanny's so it's not too hard…I sure do love them," she said as she looked at them adoringly. "Abby brings her two over to play once in awhile."

Steve smiled back at the children who were grinning through the window at him, and they shyly ran off giggling, embarrassed at their mom kissing a stranger. Then Bill dismissed the two of them with a wave of a hand and left the window too to go back to hovering around his wives cooking.

When the window was empty Steve never changed position, he still studied the window—remaining deep thought.

"What are you looking at," Nelly asked Steve curiously while trying to draw his attention away from his thoughts.

"My new readymade family," he answered as he pulled her back into his arms.

Nelly protested, "I'm too old for you!"

"Come here you old... but beautiful, of course... cougar," he teased as he held her closer and pretended to growl.

"Wait, I have something to tell you, I have my own pilots license now!" Nelly suddenly remembered to share the good news.

"OK, that's great, now shut up and let me kiss you."

****

Nelly placed the daffodils on David's grave, kissed her fingers and touched the stone. She learned in her live time that, although one can have a complete unexpected change of luck, never forget the past...it matters.

Made in the USA
Monee, IL
07 April 2021